Mark Vardy
and the
Politician's
Daughter

THE MARK VARDY SERIES

To be continued...

ISBN: 9798566300276

DEDICATION

To Rod, my Sensei, my inspiration and the original Mark Vardy.

To the memory of Sergeant David Youd, a remarkable and much loved officer and gentleman, with thanks to his family.

To all the Senseis who give so much to so many.

To my Mum, the original Lady Wallace, who made our home a castle.

In memory of my Dad, who loved Christmas.

ACKNOWLEDGMENTS

The author would like to thank Rod Walton for sharing his imagination, his Martial Arts expertise and decades of experience in the Police Force. Thank you also for the many conversations in which you helped me plan this book and your unfailing enthusiasm and belief in me.

Thank you very much to Richard Odey for his editing services. Thank you also to the friends and family of the author who so kindly read various drafts of this book and gave so much encouragement and support. Thank you to Helen Knight, Norma Goater, David Bennett, Karen Teulon, Bernard Witcher and Dawn Willock. Thank you also to Steve Fyffe and Anthony Cairns for helpful conversations.

A book like this – and those which will follow – could not have been written without so many generations of Martial Artists sharing and handing down their knowledge. I hope I have done them justice and will do so even more in the future. I must acknowledge what they have given all of us.

Finally, thank you to the New Forest, the scene of much of this book and the place of daily inspiration to the author.

Chapter 1

"Drop the Freedom of Speech Bill, or we will take your daughter."

Norman's eyes widened in shock as he read the stark threat typed on a plain white card.

"That came for you this afternoon, Sir," said his butler, Parker, as he served tea.

"Thank you, Parker," said Norman, distractedly. Parker withdrew from the library discreetly.

Norman's pulse was racing and his breath suddenly seemed short. He closed his eyes and leaned back in his chair. He knew politics was a dirty business, but this was the lowest they had sunk yet. He didn't mind facing whatever they threw at him personally, but he felt it was utterly unacceptable to bring his family into it. He also knew that he was dealing with powerful political forces who would stop at nothing to put an end to his efforts. He knew that they would do what they were threatening.

Norman pressed his lips together in a firm, determined line. He knew what he had to do. He got up and walked to the table in the library. He picked up the receiver on the telephone there and dialled a number.

***

The very next day, Norman strode purposefully over Westminster Bridge. The River Thames twinkled below and the traffic of London streamed over the bridge. Norman was a slim and immaculately neat man wearing a sober dark blue suit of impeccable quality. His hair was trimmed to a tidy, respectable style and his face carried its usual expression of indomitable determination. Norman Fairweather was a man who knew where he was going and what he was going to do. Wild horses were unlikely to dissuade him. However, central London wasn't known for herds of wild horses, so this was unlikely to be put to the test.

A little later that morning, he rose to his feet in the House of Commons. Norman Fairweather was a Member of Parliament, and today he was going to make a speech. As he stood, there were the usual jeers from both sides of the House. Norman was universally feared. He had this frustrating habit of always being right and saying the kind of things that people wished he wouldn't. Today he was going to speak on a subject that had become surprisingly controversial and dangerous.

"Honourable Members, it is my great disappointment to find that I must address you on this subject at this point in history," Norman opened his speech. The members of parliament made their usual jeering noises of disrespect. This didn't intimidate Norman even slightly though. Nothing ever did intimidate Norman, in fact. He was the kind of man who could face a herd of stampeding elephants and find that they screeched to a halt in front of him before sidling off, looking embarrassed.

He continued, "I don't think there can be a single Honourable Member who didn't grow up believing that they were free to think what they want and say what they want. Those were basic freedoms that we *all* grew up with. They were beyond question and fundamental to the concept of living in a free country."

The jeers continued even though there was no-one present who could deny the truth of what Norman was saying.

"Well, in recent times, that freedom of speech has been lost. It has been eroded by new regulations that restrict speech. It has been eroded by the media. It has been eroded here in this House. We are no longer free to say anything we would like to. If what we say offends someone, or if someone takes offence to what we say on behalf of another, the chances are that we have now broken the law.

"Now, I am not proposing that we should use the freedom of speech that we used to have to hurt other people. No decent person would do that. However, people must be free to say what they want. And other people must be free to decide if what that person says makes them an unpleasant or foolish person. The point is that we must all be free to make what judgements we may and to say whatever we would like to say.

"It is only through freedom of speech that we can hear what is really on people's minds and in their hearts. It is only in hearing from people that we can find the truth, find solutions and find peace. When people are not allowed to say what they think and feel, those thoughts and feelings do not go away. Instead, they fester, they are not discussed; they are not challenged. Peace, understanding and harmony cannot be reached without open communication.

"And even without these motivations of greater interpersonal and community harmony, the point remains that a society cannot call itself free whilst telling the public that they are not free to say whatever they think. This is a matter of freedom. Wars have been fought and won for our freedom. People have given their lives in defence of our freedom. We must treasure that freedom and stop allowing it to be eroded and destroyed, for any reason at all!"

Norman finished with a flourish and re-took his seat, pleased with his performance. There were a couple of cheers from the backbenches on one side. Mainly his speech ended in the mocking calls of those who wished simply to silence him. Norman smiled, but inside he was despairing. He had meant what he said. He was genuinely sad and surprised to find himself at a point in history where he had to make this speech. He was even more amazed that he was almost alone in valuing freedom of speech. The country had taken a worrying turn, and he feared what it would soon become.

Later that day, Norman returned home to his house in one of the nicer areas of London. It was a townhouse that ranged over five stories, complete with a basement. Painted in lemon yellow with white pillars, accents and stone balustrade, its shiny black front door had a gold letterbox and doorknob. It was a beautiful example of a London house and was presented with the same immaculate taste and attention to detail as Norman Fairweather himself.

The house had been in his family for generations. Although it was perhaps an excessively valuable house for a simple Member of Parliament to occupy, it was nevertheless a part of Norman's family history. It was also Norman's home and home to his daughter, Carlotta. It had once been a home he had shared with his wife, before she was tragically killed in a horse-riding accident.

Norman may have been a strong and obstinate man, but he was a loving and doting father. If anything, he may have been a little too indulgent with his daughter, who was as headstrong and difficult as her father. His forehead wrinkled with concern as he worried about the threat that had been made. Had he been reckless to go ahead with the speech? He sincerely hoped not.

Chapter 2

Sergeant Yeald walked along the Embankment with the deceptive pace of a police officer – appearing to move at unruffled leisure but covering the ground quickly and efficiently. It was very early on a Sunday morning, and the streets were almost empty. The sun had not long risen, and the sky was awash with a rainbow of pastel colours. Although central London was not a place one would wish to take a deep breath for much of the day, at this time the air was clear and the river swept a freshness along the Embankment where he walked. Sergeant Yeald smiled; this was his favourite time of day. In his many years as a police officer, he had experienced every part of London – from the earliest of the morning to the latest hours of the night.

They were expecting him inside the Scotland Yard building which overlooked the river. He was shown to the office of Assistant Commissioner Arthur Henderson. Arthur Henderson was a man of about fifty-five years old. He had clearly been a powerfully built warrior in his youth but now had aged to a mature frame that reminded one a little more of a very comfortable sofa. His face was still handsome, and he had the smartness of a military man.

"Alan!" cried the Assistant Commissioner. "How lovely to see you again. It's been a few years now, hasn't it?"

Sergeant Alan Yeald smiled and shook his hand. "Always a pleasure, Sir!"

"Sit down! Sit down!" The Assistant Commissioner waved toward a red leather chair with deep cushion. "Would you like a cup of tea?"

"It's always a good time for a cup of tea, dear boy!" replied Sergeant Yeald, with a broad smile as he sat down.

"I will come straight to the point," said the Assistant Commissioner. "Something has come up, something rather serious. You are aware of the Member of Parliament, Norman Fairweather?"

Sergeant Yeald nodded. "He is bringing a Bill to the House about Freedom of Speech, isn't he?"

"That's right. And that is the cause of the situation that has arisen." Assistant Commissioner Henderson's expression was grave. "He has received a threat against his young daughter, Carlotta. They have threatened to kidnap her."

"Oh, that's not on!" exclaimed Sergeant Yeald. "Not on at

all!"

The Assistant Commissioner nodded. "I am afraid it's exactly the sort of low down, cowardly strategy that we have come to expect from them over the years."

"What are we going to do about it?" asked Sergeant Yeald, who was a man of decisive action.

"I am glad you asked." The Assistant Commissioner smiled. "I am afraid it is time for us to call you back to the front line. I know you have been almost hiding out undercover as a station Sergeant in order to keep an eye on Mark Vardy and support his mother since William left us."

Sergeant Yeald nodded seriously. "I promised William I would look out for them both. He was my best friend and, of course, my colleague."

"Well, this is partly why we felt you would be the ideal man for this job that has come up," continued the Assistant Commissioner. "Mark has just been accepted at the Academy."

Sergeant Yeald gave a broad grin of pride. "Indeed he has! Good chap! He was always going to pass the selection, of course. He was born to be one of us and hasn't let us down a single moment of his short life so far. We are all so proud of him!"

"Well, this is where you come into the plan. Norman Fairweather's daughter, Carlotta, is just about the right age to join the Academy. Under normal circumstances, she is not the sort of youngster that would be selected. She is headstrong, obstinate, rebellious, difficult – everything that her father probably was at the same age. I am sure she will grow up to be a fine young woman, but for now, she is challenging. We would have a hard time keeping her well guarded here in London. But we thought she might be easier to guard and keep safe if we placed her in the Academy. She would blend in with the other students and have a more normal life there."

Sergeant Yeald laughed. "Well, it isn't exactly normal at the Academy, but I take your point!"

Assistant Commissioner gave a half nod. "Indeed, but it will be more normal than being shut inside a London house for months with only security staff for company. At least she will be with youngsters her own age at the Academy, and will be able to spend time outdoors. She might even learn a thing or two!"

"It wouldn't be the first time a young person was turned around at the Academy," said Sergeant Yeald almost wistfully, his memories crossing his face for a moment.

"We would like you to go to the Academy as Police Liaison, Alan," said the Assistant Commissioner. "This is fundamentally a close protection exercise, and we must have a Police presence on-site at the Academy to oversee things. With your history and connections with the Academy and your background in Special Branch, you would be the perfect man for the job. It will also enable you to keep an eye on Mark too. He is still a potential target, as he has always been."

Sergeant Yeald rose and shook the Assistant Commissioner's hand firmly. "I will do it. You are right. It has to be me."

Chapter 3

Sergeant Yeald was in Mark's mother's kitchen the next day when the phone rang, and the Academy told Mark that he was to return to the Academy as soon as possible.

"And so your adventures continue, young Mark!" said Sergeant Yeald.

"Isn't it brilliant?" Mark turned to him, his face alight with eagerness.

Whilst Mark flew upstairs to start packing his things, Sergeant Yeald chatted with Mark's mother. He explained that he knew all about this situation and that he would be going to the Academy for the term too.

"Tell you what – I will pick Mark up tomorrow morning and he can come down to the Academy in my car with me."

"That's very kind," replied Mark's mother. "I would feel much better knowing he is with you. And I am glad you will be there for the term. I do worry about him, you know. It's always at the back of my mind that those awful people might come for us."

"Don't you worry," assured Sergeant Yeald. "They won't get anywhere near you. And Mark's very safe at The Academy."

*

The next day, Sergeant Yeald drew up outside Mark's house in a dark green Volvo estate car. He unfolded himself from the vehicle, took Mark's suitcase and put it in the boot.

"Jump in, dear boy!" he said to Mark, who kissed his mother and then climbed into the passenger seat of the car.

"Tally ho!" he said to Mark's mother with a cheery grin and a wave.

"Let's get going! Wagons ho!" he called as he drove off. Mark's mother waved and waved until the green car disappeared around the corner at the end of the road. Mark looked over his shoulder until she was out of his sight, waving back at her.

On the way down to the Academy, Mark chattered away, nineteen to the dozen. Sergeant Yeald barely had to say a word because Mark didn't seem to stop for breath.

"Did I tell you about the motorbike chase? And the bad ninjas? And Shadowlands? It looked horrible, like a prison camp. I am so glad I went to the Academy and not there. Ooo – did I mention the White Ninja and all the light? That was amazing!

"Did I tell you about my friend? I made some brilliant new friends. My best friend there is Charlie. He is really nice. You would like him. Everyone likes Charlie. And there is David. He's from Wales. He is an excellent fellow, very decent. I know you would like him too. Oh, and there are the Scottish brothers, James and Malcolm. They come from the Highlands of Scotland. Their Dad owns a castle and a massive estate full of deer and all sorts of trees. I hope they invite me there during the holidays someday! That would be amazing!"

"Were there any girls there?" asked Sergeant Yeald, with a smile on his face, when Mark briefly paused to draw breath.

"Oh, yes. Some of my new friends are girls. There's Lucy. She's Chinese, and her Mum is a doctor at the Academy. She is great. Then there's Nell, who is a nice girl too. Oh! And there's Xinia. She is the sister of Pandora, who is totally wicked. Xinia isn't though. She's the complete opposite. We all really like her. She has a horse of her own! Oh yes – and there's Gina. Gina was a gymnast before she came to the Academy, so she is very good at things like climbing and some of the martial arts skills like break-falls and rolls."

"What were the instructors like?" asked Sergeant Yeald. "Have you got a favourite?"

"They are all my favourite because they are very kind and helpful and have lots of patience," replied Mark. He thought for a moment. "I think Sensei Goodwin might be my favourite. He tells jokes and is really nice. We were all a bit scared of Sensei Silver at first, but I think he is alright. He is just a bit scary. And there's Sensei Tanaka. He is lots of fun. He taught us Ninja Skills, which was brilliant! I wonder if there will be more Senseis when we go back?"

"Oh, I think you will find there are quite a few more for you to meet," said Sergeant Yeald, with a smile. "Now, young Mark, you are twelve now. In ten years, you will be twenty-two. Have you thought about what you would like to be and be doing when you are twenty-two?"

"I will be a policeman then," said Mark. "I will be solving

crimes and arresting bad people. I will save lives and keep the public safe." Mark paused. "I want to be like my father."

Mark looked at Sergeant Yeald and asked, "You went to the Academy with my Dad, didn't you?"

Sergeant Yeald nodded. "I did Mark."

"And you knew him when he was twenty-two as well?"

"I knew him ever since, dear boy," replied Sergeant Yeald.

Mark paused again. "What was he like? I can't remember him properly anymore. It seems so long since I last saw his face. I can't completely remember it anymore. I miss him every day, and it makes me really sad that I can't remember him properly. I feel guilty, as if that means I didn't love him. But I did! I still do!"

Mark's face was contorted with anguish for a moment. He didn't often talk about his father or his feelings. It was so much easier not to. But just sometimes his head was full of questions, and he wanted to know. Right now, he desperately hoped that Sergeant Yeald could help him remember his Dad better.

Sergeant Yeald looked at him briefly, unable to look longer because he was driving. He was quiet a moment. He wasn't a man who just spilt out the first thing that came into his head. It was more his habit to stop and think before acting or talking. He knew that what he said right now was the most important conversation he had ever had with Mark and he must get it right.

"What you are experiencing is completely normal, Mark. When we lose someone, the details of their face gradually fade in our memories. This is even more so the case for a young child. But this is all completely natural and is part of the human brain's way of adjusting to life without that loved one. The brain fades the memory to spare you pain. It doesn't mean you didn't love that person. If anything, it means you loved them so much that the brain simply had to do something to make the pain more manageable. Do you understand?"

Mark half nodded, because he only half understood.

"You will understand better in time," said Sergeant Yeald. "I can tell you that your father was the very best of men. He was tall and handsome, with black hair and blue eyes just like yours. He was athletic and powerful because he had trained so hard and for so many years at the

Academy."

"What was he like as a person?" asked Mark.

Sergeant Yeald smiled. Mark was the spitting image of his father both in appearance and character.

"He was a man of great integrity. Anyone who knew him would tell you that. He was courageous, bold and ready for any adventure. He was a kind and gentle man, but was a great warrior too. That can be hard to understand, but you will learn this at the Academy. The best of warriors are also capable of the greatest gentleness and compassion. Your father was a hero, Mark. I can't tell you all the things he did. I wish I could, dear boy. I wish I could."

"I wish he were still here." Mark blinked hard to prevent a tear. "Whenever I do something, I wish he could see it, and I wish I could tell him about it."

"He knows," replied Sergeant Yeald. "Did you know? When people die, they go to Heaven, but they can still see what their loved ones do in their lives?"

"Really? I didn't know that!" said Mark.

"Oh, yes. I promise you. Your father sees all the good

things you do, and he is very proud of you. He would have loved that rescue operation you did when you rescued the girls from Shadowlands."

Mark's face brightened at the memory of the big adventure. "Do you think so, Sir?"

Sergeant Yeald gave him a broad smile. "Absolutely dear boy. I am certain of it!"

Mark grinned, comforted at the thought and returning to happier, more recent memories. It wasn't long before his face beamed with excitement. They had arrived at the big iron gates at the entrance to The Academy. He was back!

Chapter 4

Everything was as Mark had left it a week or so ago. In his break at home, he had sometimes wondered whether his time at the Academy had been a dream. It seemed so strange and fanciful when he had told his mother about it. Yet here it was – the grand building waiting for him at the end of the long tree-lined driveway.

As the wheels of Sergeant Yeald's big car crunched on the gravel, Mark rolled down the window and stuck his head out. He breathed in the cool green-smelling air, and it felt like the whole place was welcoming him back.

He spotted Mr Liu and TigerLily in the distance. He waved madly and called, "Hello, Mr Liu! Hello, TigerLily!"

Mr Liu turned and waved with a warm smile on his face. TigerLily raised her head and tossed it briefly in greeting.

Sergeant Yeald chuckled. "Your friends are pleased to see you!"

"Oh, yes! Did I tell you? That's Mr Liu and his horse, TigerLily. She is amazing! She's such a clever horse!"

"I know Mr Liu," said Sergeant Yeald. "He has been here

at the Academy since my days."

"Wow! He must be *really* old," said Mark, amazed at the idea.

"Less of the '*old*', young man!" laughed Sergeant Yeald. "It wasn't so very long ago that I was here."

Mark laughed too. Clearly, Sergeant Yeald had very different ideas to him about what was a long time.

The car pulled up outside the front doors of The Academy, which opened as they arrived. The butler appeared and greeted them "Welcome back, Master Vardy. And welcome back to you, Sergeant Yeald! How lovely to have you with us again. The housekeeper has prepared quarters for you. Come inside, and I will show you up to them."

"Very kind, old chap, but I must go and see Professor Ballard first. Could someone take my car around, please?"

"Of course, Sir. Our driver will do that and take your bags up to your rooms."

"Jolly good! First-class, dear boy. I hope you are well?"

"Very well, Sir," replied the butler.

"Jolly good, jolly good! We will catch up later, dear boy!" With that, Sergeant Yeald ruffled Mark's hair and headed off down a nearby corridor.

Mark went straight to the Refectory, in search of a drink and with high hopes of some food. He wasn't disappointed. He found a table laid with sandwiches and cakes and pitchers of fruit juice. Tucking into this already were Charlie, Lucy and Xinia.

"Welcome back, Mark! What kept you?!" Charlie greeted Mark with a beaming smile.

"I might have known you would beat me to the cakes," laughed Mark. "Hello, everyone!"

The students were all delighted to be together again. They laughed and joked as they enjoyed their snacks. It wasn't long though before they fell on the inevitable subject.

"Why do you think they called us all back?" whispered Charlie.

"It's never happened before," said Lucy. "I have never known it happen - or even heard of it happening. There must be something very unusual going on."

28

"I am just delighted to be back!" said Xinia. "And I am so happy I could bring Rainbow back with me. I can't wait to introduce you all to him!"

"We can't wait to meet him!" cried Charlie. "You are so lucky having your own horse!"

"Can we go and see him after we finish our sandwiches?" asked Mark. He had developed an interest in horses since having an extraordinary meeting with one during the selection course. He was keen to explore the world of horses a bit more.

"Of course!" said Xinia, grabbing an apple from the table. "I think he would appreciate this." She sliced the apple into long slices and filled her pockets with them. "Let's go!"

They all followed her out, Mark and Charlie grabbing extra sandwiches to munch on their way.

Xinia led the way around the back of the main Academy building to the stable block. They entered a large square courtyard with stables arranged along all four sides, overlooking the centre. Rainbow was in one of the stables on the left.

"Everyone, I would like you to meet Rainbow!" She presented her horse with tremendous love and pride. He poked his head out of the stable, arching his neck over the stable door. He gave a low whicker of welcome to Xinia, who kissed his forehead and smoothed his shining neck. He was a grey horse but was so pale and luminous, he looked the colour of silver.

"Rainbow, this is Mark – and Charlie – and you already met Lucy, of course."

"Wow! He is absolutely magnificent!" said Mark. He reached out to him slowly, not looking him straight in the eyes so as not to alarm him. Rainbow bowed his head and allowed Mark to stroke his forehead and forelock gently.

Charlie was keen to stroke Rainbow too. "May I?" he asked Rainbow. Rainbow turned his head to Charlie and gently nudged his arm. Charlie giggled and stroked his neck.

They stood there a little while, Mark on one side of Rainbow's head and Charlie on the other. Lucy lent forward and kissed Rainbow's velvet-soft nose.

Xinia smiled. It made her very happy to see her friends

getting to know her beloved horse and for him to be so pleased to meet them.

Chapter 5

Mark and his friends all gathered back in the Refectory for the evening meal at six o'clock. By then, all the other students had arrived, and there was further excitement and speculation about their early summons back to the Academy. They didn't have to wait long, though. The door opened and in walked Professor Ballard, along with several other Senseis, Sergeant Yeald and a strange-looking girl of around their age.

The students all rose to their feet when the Senseis came in. The little procession lined up on the low stage on which sat the High Table where the Senseis usually ate their meals. Professor Ballard gestured to the students to take their seats before he addressed them.

"Welcome back to the Academy. Thank you for responding to our request that you return early. I expect some of you will be aware that this is an extremely unusual thing to happen. In fact, it is unprecedented. But it has been done for a very important reason, which I am sure you will understand.

"You may be aware of the Member of Parliament, Norman Fairweather. Mr Fairweather is currently trying to introduce a Bill in the House of Commons which will safeguard the right of all British people to freedom of speech."

The students looked at each other blankly. The notion of freedom of speech was a new one to most of them. Mark and Charlie grinned at each other. They were both outspoken boys who felt fairly free in their speech already!

Professor Ballard smiled indulgently. "Yes, yes. I don't suppose you are old enough to understand about this yet." His voice grew more serious. "It is a matter of great importance though. A country is not truly free unless its people are free to think as they wish and speak as they wish. Freedom of speech is a core freedom in a free country. As young people, you probably haven't experienced anyone telling you that you can't say certain things. But the time will come, as you grow older. You will find there are certain words you can't use, certain ideas you can't talk about and certain opinions you can't voice. It shouldn't be that way. It didn't use to be that way. But the world has changed, and there are forces at work in this country – bad, dark, forces – which seek to take away your freedom one piece at a time. If they can control what you say, they will eventually control what you think. Then they will control what you do. Then there will be no freedom left at all.

"You may be wondering what this has to do with you and why you have been called back to the Academy so soon. Well, I would like to introduce you to someone." He gestured to the strange-looking girl. She had long black hair that fell in a wild cloud down her back. It was streaked with purple, which matched her purple and black eye makeup. Her clothes were similarly unusual. She wore ripped black jeans with a short tartan skirt over the top and a slashed Tshirt with metal fixings. Altogether, she did not look anything like the kind of young person that the Academy normally recruited.

"This is Carlotta Fairweather, the daughter of the Member of Parliament, Mister Norman Fairweather. Because of her father's work to protect freedom of speech, threats have been made against Carlotta's safety. So we have agreed to take Carlotta into the Academy to protect her whilst her father does his work. Carlotta will become a student here and mix in with all of you in order to keep her hidden."

The students looked at each other, doubtfully. This girl didn't look like she could mix in anywhere without being noticed. It certainly didn't seem likely that she could be hidden amongst them at the Academy.

Professor Ballard picked up their doubts. "Obviously, a few changes will have to be made..." his voice trailed off. "Now I would like Carlotta to join you for dinner. Please make her welcome and help her fit in." He waved Carlotta over to the students' table.

Xinia and Lucy shuffled aside to make room for her between them at the table. Carlotta was grateful but was too cool to let on that she had been feeling a bit of an outsider.

Professor Ballard wasn't finished, though. "I would also like to introduce you to Sergeant Yeald. Sergeant Yeald is a real police officer with extremely extensive experience that covers many areas. He is here to act as police liaison between the Academy and Special Branch. He will help us and lead us in our mission to keep Carlotta safe. So you must all listen to him and obey him at all times. If you are wise, you will take the opportunity to learn all that you can from him.

"You are very lucky. Normally our students would not learn about bodyguarding until much later in their training. You are going to start learning now, though. You are all here because you have proven yourselves on the selection course and gone beyond all expectations when you performed a rescue mission in the final assessment. That is why we feel confident to trust you with this task. You must do your best and remember that this isn't a game. A young lady's welfare and life may depend on it."

With this warning, Professor Ballard left them to their dinner and took his seat at the High Table with Sergeant Yeald and the other Senseis.

Chapter 6

"Hello, Carlotta. I'm Mark, and this is Charlie, Lucy, Xinia, David, James, Malcolm, Gina and Nell." Mark introduced everyone, and they all nodded and waved to Carlotta as their names were mentioned.

"Hello," said Carlotta, a little shyly. Despite her outrageous appearance, Carlotta could be a little shy before she got to know people. Right now, she was in a strange environment, away from her home and everything familiar. She was also a well brought up young lady and knew her manners, even if she didn't always choose to deploy them. On this occasion, she decided to though. "I am pleased to meet you. Thank you for having me here."

"It's our pleasure!" cried Charlie. "We are really excited to become your bodyguards!"

All the students nodded eagerly. "You will be safe with us," said David in his light welsh accent. Carlotta looked at the strong, determined Welsh lad and believed him. These seemed like friendly people, and there were certainly a lot of people here who wanted to be her bodyguard!

"We are going to have to do something about your

appearance though Carlotta," said Lucy. "You stand out like a sore thumb at the moment."

"I think your hair is beautiful," said Nell.

"It's really cool!" agreed Gina.

"But it will have to change," said Xinia, "Or you will be a very easy target for potential kidnappers."

"We could sort you out after dinner," suggested Lucy.

Carlotta felt reluctant, but she understood what needed to happen and why. Underneath it all, she was quite frightened of getting kidnapped. Carlotta knew her father had a lot of enemies and that there was a big fight going on at the moment in the world of politics. She dreaded to think who might try and take her and what they would do with her. Under the circumstances, changing her hair was a small price to pay. Besides, it would be just a temporary disguise.

"Okay," she said, jutting her chin out to try and look a bit more determined and in control of her situation than she actually felt.

They all tucked into their dinner, which was a lovely stir

fry of vegetables and bean curd in a delicate lemongrass and garlic sauce. There were spring rolls and crackers too, and a tasty sweetcorn soup as a starter. Desert was a confection of deep-fried banana chunks in a toffee sesame sauce, topped with coconut ice cream and drizzled with chocolate sauce. Carlotta decided that it was worth coming to the Academy for the food alone!

After dinner, the girls all went up to Lucy and Xinia's room. It was the largest of the girl's rooms and now had an additional bed and cupboard in it for Carlotta. "They thought it was safest to put you in with us," said Lucy. Carlotta could see the logic, although she would have preferred a room to herself.

"Now, let's see about your hair," said Xinia, looking closely. "Those purple streaks will have to go. We might have to take you to a hairdresser to get them dyed."

"It's ok, they are just clip-in hair pieces," said Carlotta. She unclipped one and removed it. The purple hair came away and fell from a small clip that she now held in her hand.

"Ah! That's handy!" said Gina, thinking she might like some clip-in hair colours herself.

Carlotta carefully unclipped all her purple streaks until she was left with just her natural long black hair. Lucy looked at her thoughtfully a moment, then at Xinia, then back to Carlotta.

"I have an idea," she said. "Take your makeup off."

Carlotta pouted. This was a step too far.

Lucy put her hands on her hips and raised an eyebrow. "We are trying to help you."

Carlotta relented. She was right. They were all trying to help, and she knew she couldn't continue to wear her wild makeup whilst she was here. It was time to take off the mask and perhaps find a new one to wear. She got up, went to her bag and fished around inside it. Then she pulled out some makeup removing fluid, cotton wool and a facecloth. She went to the little sink and mirror in the corner of the room and removed her makeup. When she turned around and faced the others, she looked like a different girl!

"Just as I thought!" said Lucy. "You look really like Xinia!"

Xinia went to Carlotta, and they stood side by side facing

the mirror. There was a resemblance. Carlotta's hair was longer, black and had a natural wave to it whereas Xinia's was dark brown and straight. Xinia had a fringe whereas Carlotta didn't. But that could be easily changed. The girls smiled – they could make themselves look very similar if they wanted.

"This could come in handy," said Xinia. "Let's go to the hairdresser in the village tomorrow and see what they can do to make us look more alike. Then the bad people would have an even harder job spotting you amongst us!

"Brilliant idea!" said Gina. Lucy and Nell nodded and agreed.

"Will you do it?" asked Lucy.

Carlotta and Xinia grinned. "Yes," they both said. "It will be fun! We will both be in disguise!"

Chapter 7

When the girls explained their plan to Professor Ballard and Sergeant Yeald, they agreed that it was a good one. And so morning lessons were suspended so that the girls could go to the village and visit the hairdresser.

The boys decided that hairdressing was for girls and not something they wanted to get involved with. So they stayed at the Academy and spent the morning exploring the grounds once more. It was such a big place, and they had only seen a small part of it when they had been here for the selection course.

Mark and Charlie went looking for Mr Liu. They soon found him in the rose garden, weeding the flower beds with a long hoe. TigerLily wandered along beside him, nibbling at the grass.

"Hello, Mr Liu! Hello, TigerLily!" both boys called out in greeting. Mr Liu turned and smiled. He was delighted to see them. TigerLily gave them a low whicker of welcome and went back to grazing.

"Welcome back!" said Mr Liu. "Welcome, welcome!"

"We are so happy to be back," said Mark. "And we have a new adventure! We are going to be bodyguards! Did they tell you?"

"Ah yes, I know," said Mr Liu. "And very fine bodyguards you will make if your previous exploits are anything to judge by!"

"We have to guard Carlotta and prevent her from getting kidnapped," said Charlie, with great excitement. "Will you help us?"

"Of course!" said Mr Liu, "and TigerLily will!"

The boys grinned. This was going to be great!

"Where are the girls?" asked Mr Liu "I haven't met Carlotta yet."

"They went into the village to do something with their hair," said Mark dismissively. What girls did with their hair was of very little interest to him, and he didn't see what it had to do with being bodyguards. But Professor Ballard had allowed it, so there was probably a reason.

Mr Liu chuckled. "Girls will be girls!...And boys will be boys!" he added.

Mark and Charlie grinned. "I can't believe we are back here," said Mark. "It seemed like a dream once I got home and I was telling Mum about it."

"We are right at the beginning of our story now," said Charlie. "From here on, we will train to become the best warriors in the world, and we will have the most fantastic adventures and become proper heroes!"

"I am sure you will," said Mr Liu. "In fact, I am certain of it." He winked. "I know these things!"

Both the boys' faces lit up with beaming smiles. They were so excited about everything that would happen and the life that stretched ahead of them!

Chapter 8

By lunchtime, the girls had returned from their mission to the hairdressers. Mark and Charlie met them on their way back up the long gravelled drive.

"Wow!" cried Charlie.

"Goodness!" said Mark. The boys looked from Xinia to Carlotta and back again. They were almost exactly alike. Xinia's hair had been dyed black to match Carlotta's and Carlotta had had a fringe cut to match Xinia's. The only difference was that Carlotta's hair had a slight wave to it. The hairdresser had straightened it, but the rebellious waves were making a determined return in the moisture of the air.

"I can barely tell you apart!" said Charlie.

"That's the idea!" exclaimed Lucy. "If they look the same, then the kidnappers won't be able to tell which one is Carlotta. So they won't be able to kidnap her! Simple!"

The boys agreed that this was an excellent idea. "What made you think of that?" asked Mark, who was always curious about how people came to decisions.

"Well, once we started trying to transform Carlotta into an Academy student, I noticed how similar their faces are," said Lucy. "Then it was just a matter of a bit of hairdressing, as you see..."

"That's brilliant!" said Mark. "It will make you much easier to bodyguard."

Carlotta flashed him a brief smile. "I am glad you think so."

They all poured into the main building and went straight to the Refectory for a lunch of sandwiches, crisps and juice. Over lunch, Carlotta fitted in with the other students much more easily. After their hairdressing expedition and spending time with the other girls, she felt much more like one of them. The other girls had been very kind and welcoming too, which had helped. She began to think that this time at the Academy wouldn't be so bad after all. At least everyone was nice to her.

"Thank you all for being so welcoming to me," said Carlotta.

"You are welcome", "Our pleasure", "Not at all" came the replies.

"I have never been to school before," said Carlotta. "I didn't realise it could be so nice."

"You've never been to school?" questioned Charlie, with amazement. All the students looked surprised and confused. Carlotta was surely old enough to have been at school for many years by now.

"No. I was educated at home before now. My father used to employ governesses and tutors to teach me." replied Carlotta, a little embarrassed at being different from the other students.

"So you didn't have any school friends?" asked Gina, who found this hard to imagine.

"No, not really. Well, I had some sort of friends – children of my father's friends. But that was different. I didn't see them very often."

"You must have been lonely," said Xinia, sympathetically.

"It was all I have known," said Carlotta. "But I am beginning to realise that maybe I was, yes."

"Well, we will be your friends now," said Mark. "You need never feel lonely again."

Carlotta smiled gratefully. All the other students nodded and smiled too.

"I am going to like it here," said Carlotta.

Chapter 9

After lunch, the students reported to the Summer Dojo. They were expecting their first Martial Arts lesson since coming back, with Sensei Goodwin. Sensei Goodwin greeted them at the doors of the dojo and welcomed them inside. Waiting for them there was Sergeant Yeald.

"Hello, boys and girls!" said the Sergeant.

"Hello, Sergeant Yeald" they all chorused back.

Sensei Goodwin smiled at them all. "Welcome back!" He made the formal bow of the dojo to them, and they all returned it.

"You have all met Sergeant Yeald," said Sensei Goodwin. "I am going to leave you in his capable hands this afternoon to learn the basics of bodyguarding. Listen well and learn all that you can. As you will have realised by now, this is all very real."

With that warning, Sensei Goodwin made another brief bow, which the students returned, before leaving the dojo.

"Well then," said Sergeant Yeald. "Do we have any bodyguards here?" He walked up and down the line of students, inspecting each one as he went. He appeared to be looking for signs of bodyguards. Mark and Charlie stood to attention and tried to imagine what bodyguards stood like so they could look like them.

"Hands up if you are a bodyguard!" said Sergeant Yeald. He looked along the line again. No hands went up.

"There are no bodyguards here? I am amazed!" he paused a moment, playing with his eager audience.

"There must be something wrong with your eyesight. I can see ten bodyguards in front of me!"

The students all looked at each other, not quite understanding. Mark and Charlie began to feel somewhat satisfied. Clearly their attempts to stand like bodyguards had been at least a little successful.

Sergeant Yeald chuckled. "You are all bodyguards! You are all responsible for protecting the most important body of all – your own!"

The students all laughed with relief, understanding what he was saying at last.

"You must learn to protect yourself before you can protect

others. Your first bodyguarding client is yourself. Now everything you have been learning in your Martial Arts lessons is part of that protection. But there are other lessons to learn. Bodyguarding goes beyond simply fighting and physically defending yourselves. In fact, if it gets to that, then something has gone wrong in your plan – probably many things have."

The students listened in rapt attention. He gestured to them to sit down on the matt. There was a lot of talking to be done!

"The first thing you must learn about bodyguarding is the art of awareness. We have a colour scale to help describe this, a bit like the colours of traffic lights. We start in one colour and then progress to the next as the situation unfolds."

Charlie tilted his head to one side, not quite understanding all this yet. Sergeant Yeald picked up his confusion and that of the others.

"Most people walk around in White. That means they are completely oblivious to the potential dangers that surround them. They are not paying attention. If something bad happens, it would be a complete surprise to them. A bodyguard is never in White. A martial artist should never be in White also. You must always be aware of your surroundings and alert to possible dangers."

Nell looked a bit unhappy about this. She raised her hand. Sergeant Yeald nodded to her, indicating that she should speak. "Wouldn't that mean we are always feeling frightened, Sir?"

"Oh no! Not at all!" said Sergeant Yeald. "The point of being aware is that you know when there could be a problem and when it is unlikely that there will be one. You need never feel frightened of anything when you can do that. In fact, you should feel frightened if you are not aware of what is going on around you because that is when you are vulnerable. You are being trained to become first-class martial artists. It won't be long before you are able to defend yourself competently in any situation. "

Nell's eyes lit up. She liked the sound of that. She often found herself feeling nervous or frightened. She worried about bad things happening. She liked the idea of never having to worry again!

Sergeant Yeald continued. "A bodyguard is always in at least Yellow state. He – or she – is aware of his surroundings. He knows who is there, what is there and what could potentially become a problem. He is always looking, scanning, searching. He is always aware and paying attention. This is called Mental Alertness.

"Now if you do detect something in your environment or situation that makes you think there is a possibility of danger, you go into Amber. This means that you are ready to take action. If you can, you take yourselves away from the situation. If you are guarding another, you take them away from it too."

Mark's hand shot up. Sergeant Yeald nodded. "What if you can't get away, Sir?"

"I am glad you asked that dear boy!" replied Sergeant Yeald. "If you can't get away, that's when you will have to fight to defend yourself – and your Principal."

"Our Principal? What, Professor Ballard?" asked Charlie, confused. "Why would he be there?"

Sergeant Yeald roared with laughter. "No! Your Principal is the person you are guarding. That's what we call it in bodyguarding – the Principal."

All the students laughed. Charlie laughed too.

After the laughter subsided, Sergeant Yeald returned to his lesson.

"When you go into fighting mode, it is said that you have gone into Red."

"Are there any colours after Red?" asked David, having raised his hand politely, as the other's had.

"Yes, the last colour is Black. You don't want to reach Black," said Sergeant Yeald.

Charlie's hand shot up again. Sergeant Yeald shook his head. He knew what the question would be.

"If you reach Black, it means you are dead. It means that you lost the fight. It means that your entire bodyguarding strategy has failed. We do everything we can to avoid reaching Black," he said gravely.

The students looked shocked now. Their earlier laughter was completely wiped from their faces. It hadn't occurred to them that this is what could happen.

"So now you understand what a serious business this is,"

said Sergeant Yeald. "Which is why it is essential to pay attention to the earlier stages, have good plans and be well trained. You mustn't worry. That's what we are going to start doing now."

Sergeant Yeald then went on to teach them what he called the "box system". He asked Carlotta to stand in the middle. Then he asked James and Malcolm to stand in two corners of a square in front of her and Gina and Xinia in two corners behind her. The four of them formed a box around her. He directed Mark to stand next to Carlotta.

"You are the chief bodyguard in this situation, Mark. The other four forming this box are your bodyguarding team. Carlotta is your Principal." He shot a look at Charlie, who giggled.

"Now then," said Sergeant Yeald, "we are going to do an exercise. I want Carlotta to walk around the dojo, with the four box guards holding the frame and Mark at her side. Then, I want the remaining students to act as potential attackers. You are to be walking around in the opposite direction and when I point to you, I want you to try and attack Carlotta. Obviously..." he paused to make sure he was understood. "Obviously I don't want you to actually hurt each other. This is just a training exercise. So your objective will be to simply tap Carlotta on the shoulder. If you can do that, then the bodyguards have failed. Bodyguard team – you should simply wrestle the attackers to the mats. Don't hurt them. Remember, these are your training partners, not real attackers. I will be very unhappy if anyone gets hurt today!

"Now this is the important point. Mark, you are Carlotta's chief bodyguard. So when there is an incoming attack, it is your job to get her to safety if possible. You shouldn't be staying to fight if it is possible to get her away. Do you understand?"

"Yes, Sir!" said Mark brightly, excited and proud to be the first one to be picked to play the chief bodyguard.

The students acted out the scenario as directed by Sergeant Yeald. Carlotta walked around the dojo, and the team held their box formation around her. Then Sergeant Yeald pointed to Charlie, who launched a spirited attack through the front of the box formation. James caught him and wrestled him to the ground. Then Sergeant Yeald pointed to David, who attacked the formation from behind. As Xinia wrestled him to the mats, Mark grabbed Carlotta's arm and dragged her quickly away and to the dojo door.

"Stop!" called Sergeant Yeald. "Very good! Exactly what I asked for. I can see you have the hang of this. Don't worry – we will practise this a lot. It is a core bodyguarding skill."

"Mark, do you know why I stopped you there?" he asked.

"No, Sir" replied Mark, wondering what he had done wrong.

"Well, you got it perfectly right up until this point. You kept her within the box for the first threat, which was well handled. But when the second threat came in, you judged that it was time to get your Principal away. That was excellent judgement!"

Mark beamed. It had all felt very instinctive and natural to him. He just knew the point where it was time to get Carlotta away. But what had he done wrong?

"You were about to take her out of the dojo door, weren't you?" asked Sergeant Yeald.

"Yes, Sir," Mark nodded.

"Well, that isn't something to do lightly. Taking a Principal through a door is always a time for concern and taking her out of the building requires it's own risk assessment. Do you know why?"

Mark thought a moment. "Because there might be someone outside?"

"Exactly so, dear boy!" exclaimed Sergeant Yeald. "You don't know who is out there. They may have even set up the attack situation in here to drive Carlotta outside where they can attack or capture her."

"Doors and exits are a lesson for another day, though. Let's practise this exercise a few more times so that everyone can have a go at playing chief bodyguard, bodyguard team and Principal."

Chapter 10

By the end of the afternoon, the students' heads were swimming with bodyguarding information. Sergeant Yeald dismissed them an hour before dinner, so they had some leisure time.

"Let's take Carlotta to meet Mr Liu," suggested Charlie.

"Who is Mr Liu?" asked Carlotta, curious to know who this man that the students kept mentioning was.

"He's the gardener," said Mark. "You will really like him. He is very kind and wise. He has been here at the Academy for decades!"

The gang of ten strolled across the lawns, in search of Mr Liu. They found him at the side of the main building, doing something in the flower beds there. He appeared to be tying bits of a plant to a wooden frame. Looking curiously over his shoulder was TigerLily.

Carlotta squealed with horror. "It's a horse!" she said.

The others turned and looked at her in surprise at her reaction. "Yes, that's TigerLily," said Xinia. "TigerLily is Mr Liu's companion."

"I don't like horses," said Carlotta, backing away as Mr Liu turned around. Mr Liu saw her fear. He whispered to TigerLily, laid a hand on TigerLily's broad chest a moment and then walked towards the students, whilst TigerLily stayed where he had left her. He had clearly asked TigerLily to remain behind.

"Hello," said Mr Liu. "You must be Carlotta, our new guest."

"Yes Sir, I am," said Carlotta, trying to be polite but shooting wary glances at TigerLily.

"You are afraid of horses?" asked Mr Liu. "Why is that?"

"My mother was killed by a horse," said Carlotta sadly.

"I am very sorry to hear that," said Mr Liu. "I can understand why you might be afraid. May I ask what happened?" Mr Liu suspected that Carlotta's mother hadn't been intentionally killed by a horse as this was an incredibly unusual thing to happen.

"She had a riding accident. A car drove past her too fast when she was riding on the road one day. Her horse spooked and went sideways into the path of another car.

That car hit her horse, and she came off. The horse landed on top of her, and she died." Carlotta explained in surprising detail and with remarkable coolness.

"Ah, I see," said Mr Liu. "So the horse didn't intend to hurt anyone. But bad things happened, and your mother died. I am so very sorry to hear that. Don't let it put you off horses though. It would be a shame to live a life without knowing horses when you have the opportunity to do so."

"I can't help it," said Carlotta. "I know it wasn't the horse's fault, but every time I see one, my heart races and I want to run away."

"That's understandable," said Mr Liu. "Well if you want to try and change how you feel, TigerLily would be very happy to help you. She is a very good and clever horse. She would never hurt you."

"Thank you, Mr Liu," said Carlotta. "Maybe one day."

"When the time is right, you will find your courage," said Mr Liu. "Don't worry; the time will come."

Carlotta made a little bow, just as she had been taught in the dojo. Mr Liu smiled and returned her bow.

Chapter 11

The next day, the students returned to the Summer Dojo. This time Sensei Goodwin greeted them and said that he would be teaching the lesson and it would be about self-defence.

"Let's start with a recap of the blocking you did in your selection course. There are ten of you, so you should be able to form five pairs. Charlie, you pair up with Carlotta and teach her the blocking that you were taught. The rest of you can practise."

He wandered around, watching the pairs as they practised. "Very good! I see you all remembered. Carlotta – that's good. Make sure you protect your head all the time. Heads are vital, and we try very hard not to let them get hit!"

After a while, he called them back to order, and they lined up on the edge of the dojo. "I am going to teach you a new technique now. It is called the Pluck, and it comes from the Krav Maga system."

He looked along the line of students to select the biggest of them as his demonstration assistant, or "uke" as he called them. "David, you can be uke for this. I want you to stand in front of me and try to strangle me."

David stepped forward. He felt a bit unsure about strangling his instructor, but he was inclined to follow orders and trusted Sensei Goodwin knew what he was asking him to do. He reached out and clasped his hands onto Sensei Goodwin's throat. In a flash, Sensei Goodwin had plucked his hands away and stepped back out of reach. It happened so fast that all the class gasped. Sensei Goodwin laughed "Effective, isn't it?"

"That was brilliant," cried Charlie, enthusiastically.

"I will do it again slowly so you can see how it is done." Sensei Goodwin nodded to David to strangle him again. This time Sensei Goodwin moved very slowly. "See, I swoop my arms around and then sharply pluck David's arms away. I don't wrestle with them. If you are weaker, you will lose if you try and wrestle the arms away. It has to be a hard, sharp pluck. And once you have done that, you must step back immediately, so he doesn't fall forward and headbutt you. He might not intend to, but if you have plucked his hands away, he can easily just fall forward. So just step back smartly just after you pluck so that you are free of the strangle and not likely to get headbutted. Do you think you can do that? Come on then, get into pairs and give it a go!"

The students paired up and tried the technique. Some of them managed it immediately. Some of them fell into the mistake of trying to wrestle or simply pull the strangling arms away.

"Pluck!" called Sensei Goodwin, wandering the room and seeing the usual mix of mistakes and successes. "Pluck! Pluck! Pluck! Don't make me sound like a chicken!" he chuckled. The students laughed. As they practised the technique, they started saying "Pluck!" as they did so.

"There seem to be a lot of chickens in here!" said Sensei Goodwin. "But at least you aren't wrestling with each other any more. Now change partners and see what it is like doing this technique on different sized people. I think you will find this becomes one of your favourite techniques. It always works – well, almost always. If you ever find yourself in this attack and the person trying to strangle you is so very much stronger than you that you think it won't work, then give him a swift kick in the shins, and you will find that the technique works very well. The moment you kick him in the shins, he is going to be thinking about how much that hurt and his grip on your neck will loosen."

Sensei Goodwin paused. "But remember, we have to be quite sure that the force we use is reasonable. You will have a lesson with Sergeant Yeald this afternoon on the subject of reasonable force. When you come back tomorrow, you can tell me if is it reasonable to kick the shin of someone who is trying to strangle you or not!"

The lesson went on after that. Sensei Goodwin revised many of the things they had done on the selection course. They practised two-handed blocks, breakaways, the break-falls they had learned before and many other self-defence based martial art techniques. Carlotta was new to it all of course, but she soon caught up. She was surprised to find that she rather enjoyed the martial arts lesson. She had never done anything like it before. She also found it reassuring to learn techniques to defend herself. That might come in rather handy in the weeks and months ahead.

Chapter 12

After lunch, the students returned to the Summer Dojo for their lesson with Sergeant Yeald.

"Welcome! Welcome! Come in and take a seat," he said, with a big welcoming smile. It had been some years since he had last taught, and he was rather enjoying himself. Sergeant Yeald liked young people and privately felt rather privileged to be training the police officers, soldiers and agents of the next generation. He was keen to pass on his knowledge and instil the right kind of values.

As the students settled, he started his lesson. "Today, I am going to talk to you about the law. Specifically, I am going to talk to you about the law regarding self-defence. You are fortunate young people. You are receiving the very best of martial arts training here at the Academy. However, it won't be long before you are potentially extremely dangerous. You are learning techniques that could really hurt people. So you need to know when you can legally and morally use what you have been taught. With great power comes great responsibility."

He paused and looked at them seriously, searching their faces for acknowledgement and understanding of what he was saying. He could see ten young faces looking back at him with a mixture of eagerness, excitement and solemnity. He knew that they understood what he was telling them.

"There are two elements to what I want to teach you – what you can legally do and what you can morally do. Very often, these are the same thing as the law is well designed in this area. But occasionally there will be a situation where you must call on a higher morality to restrain you. That is a more difficult subject. But we will start with the law today.

"Now, does anyone know how much force you can use to defend yourself?"

Mark's hand shot up.

"Is there anyone other than Mark who knows this? I know you do Mark!" he asked. There were no hands initially. "Does anyone want to take a guess?"

Charlie put his hand up.

"Yes, Charlie?"

"Can you just do whatever you have to?"

The other students laughed. That sounded like far too simple a description to them.

"Well, you aren't far wrong, Charlie. In fact, you are more or less right in the grand scheme of things. Mark, do you want to tell everyone?" Seargent Yeald invited.

"A person may use reasonable force in defence of himself or another," recited Mark, who had been taught many snippets of law by his father and Seargent Yeald over the years. He also had his father's copy of the policeman's handbook, which he consulted regularly and had been memorising since he was very young.

"Excellent, Mark!" said Seargent Yeald. "Now, can anyone tell me what constitutes reasonable force?"

Charlie's hand went up again. "Doing whatever you have to!"

"Well, yes," said Sergeant Yeald. "It means doing what is necessary and what is proportionate. The next question is 'Proportionate to what?'"

"Proportionate to what they did?" asked Charlie.

"Well, they might not have done anything yet," said

Sergeant Yeald. "It has to be proportionate to the harm that would otherwise be done. So if someone says they are going to slap you and they raise their hand to do so, is it reasonable to break their leg?"

"No!" roared the class, laughing.

"What might be proportionate?" asked Sergeant Yeald

"Blocking and slapping him instead?" asked Mark.

"Well, that would depend on who was about to slap you. If it was your six-year-old little sister, would it be reasonable to slap her if she threatened to slap you?"

The students had mixed responses to this. Some thought it would be reasonable; others didn't.

"Put it this way. If you were in court and had been charged with assaulting your six your old sister, would you be able to convince a jury that it was necessary and proportionate to slap her instead?"

The students thought a moment. They all shook their heads, realising that this would be a tough argument to make.

"So, we have to consider who it is we are defending ourselves against. And we have to consider our own vulnerabilities too. These things are called Impact Factors. It's all pretty much common sense really. A little old lady might have to use more force to defend herself against a fit young man than another fit young man might. And as young people of your age, with your size and strength, it wouldn't be reasonable to use a lot of force on a small child. It might not be reasonable to use any in fact. If I were you, I would just let your baby sister slap you and leave it to your parents to talk to her about it.

"I know it all sounds rather complicated, but it comes down to this: You must always act with a good heart. That means you don't hurt people any more than you have to in order to stay safe. And you never hurt people to punish them or in retribution. That's not what self-defence is for, and you would not be protected under the law if you were to do that.

"Now then, let's imagine some scenarios and work out what is reasonable force and what isn't. Whenever you train in future, I want you to think about when it would be reasonable to use the techniques you are taught and when it wouldn't be. I want to hear you ask this question after every scenario: Was that reasonable?"

Chapter 13

The students woke the next morning to a beautiful autumn morning. They were full of excitement because today was the day they would have their first Ninja horse riding lesson. They ate their breakfast at speed, and every one of them turned up at the stable yard early for their class - everyone except Carlotta that was. Carlotta went to see Professor Ballard to explain that she couldn't possibly attend this lesson because she was afraid of horses.

"We know of your particular circumstances and your difficulties with horses. You won't be asked to ride today, but please go and watch the lesson and join in with what you can of it," Professor Ballard urged her. "You might need some of this one day."

So Carlotta went along to the lesson, quite determined that nothing would induce her to touch a horse. It wouldn't harm to watch, though.

Her fears turned out to be entirely unnecessary. Sensei Tanaka greeted the students. "Ah! Welcome back, my little ninjas! Today we learn how to get on a horse!"

The students looked confused. There were no horses

around. They were all out in the fields that stretched into the distance behind the stable yard.

Sensei Tanaka chuckled. "Horse riding is an essential Ninja skill! Getting on the horse is an essential horse riding skill! But no horse is needed!"

Mark and Charlie exchanged doubtful looks.

This highly amused Sensei Tanaka, who was enjoying teasing his class. "Follow me!" he said and set off at his usual smart pace.

The students knew how easy it was to lose Sensei Tanaka. He had somewhat of a habit of disappearing into thin air when it pleased him. They hurried to keep up with him. He took them through the stable yard and out to the fields, where the horses could be seen at the far end.

"Do we have to catch them first, Sensei?" asked Charlie, who hadn't quite grasped the idea of learning to mount a horse without actually having a horse to mount.

"No! No need to catch! Fence rails don't run away!" Sensei Tanaka chuckled. "Watch!"

He placed one foot on the bottom rail of the fence and then

swung his other leg up and over the fence so that he sat astride it. "Simple!" he said, before demonstrating a similar dismount from the fence.

"You want us to practise on the fence, Sensei?" asked Mark, surprised.

"Yes! Your turn! Everybody, mount the fence!" Sensei Tanaka issued the order with a flourish, indicating that there was a wide expanse of fence for them to practise on.

The students all thought this a rather strange direction, but they knew better than to question it further. They all started trying to mount the fence.

Gina, being a very fit and agile gymnast, found this very easy. She put a foot on the fence and swung herself up onto the top rail with the lightness and control of a cat. Some of the other students struggled a bit to pull themselves up. Some of the boys attacked the task with too much power and performed rather harsh, clumpy manoeuvres.

Sensei Tanaka wandered up and down the fence, observing their efforts. "Again! And again! And again! You must practise using your muscles to perform this movement. You must teach them to spring easily and lightly up.

Horse's backs are more delicate than they look. You mustn't bounce and pull at them. So we learn to mount here, and we train our muscles to mount lightly and gently. This is just another technique, like your martial arts techniques. You are training your muscle memory. That involves a lot of repetitions!"

The students continued trying. After half a dozen attempts, they were growing weary and getting a bit fed up with it. Sensei Tanaka stopped them a moment and asked Gina to demonstrate the task. She did so very well again.

"See Gina! See how light and controlled she is. You must do this like Gina!"

More of this exercise followed. Sensei Tanaka was determined to train this task well. Eventually, he relented and gave them another break. "Enough! For now. Follow me!"

He led them to a grassed area behind the stable block. Set up here were half a dozen wooden horses. They were the size of real horses, but their legs were made of wooden poles that were set deep in the ground. This made them very stable and able to withstand the kind of exercises that followed.

"You don't always have a saddle. We often ride without saddles. So this means you must get on the horse without a stirrup to help you step up."

Sensei Tanaka then demonstrated a couple of different techniques for mounting a horse without a saddle. One involved quite literally leaping onto the horse by swinging his leg over the horse's back from the ground as he leapt. Somehow he ended up on top of the horse. The students all looked very impressed at this.

Sensei Tanaka sat on the wooden horse a moment. "This is a more difficult way. You must have a good strong jump to do this. I will show you an easier way."

With that, he swung his leg over the back of the wooden horse and landed lightly on the ground. Then he faced the side of the horse, placed his hands on the top of the horse's back and jumped so that he was laying over the horse's back. Then he swung his leg around and over the back of the horse until he was once again sitting upright there.

"This one is slower," he said. "But try them both and see which you can learn to do. We have all morning!"

The students looked at each other. It was going to be a long morning!

"And when you have mastered that, you will learn to pull a second rider up behind you from the ground. This is a most excellent ninja skill and important for making a quick getaway!"

By lunchtime, the students were exhausted and aching. Sensei Tanaka had worked them hard, determined to teach them these skills. Many of them were very disappointed that they hadn't got to see any horses, other than the ones that watched them with mild interest from the paddock nearby.

"I really wanted to ride today," said Mark.

"Me too!" added Charlie.

"I wanted a cuddle with a horse," said Nell, sad that she hadn't had the opportunity today. She had been really looking forward to it.

"You can come and cuddle Rainbow if you would like," offered Xinia. "Rainbow loves cuddles!"

Nell perked up. "Yes, please! That would be lovely!"

"Well, I am glad there weren't any real horses today," said Carlotta. "I don't mind wooden ones!"

They all giggled. "Why don't you come and meet Rainbow?" suggested Xinia. "He would be in the stable, so you don't have to get any closer than you feel happy to."

"Thank you, but I don't think so," said Carlotta. She didn't want to hurt Xinia's feelings, but the idea did not appeal to her at all.

"All the more horsey cuddles for me then!" said Nell with a grin.

"If we hurry, there is just enough time for us to go and see Rainbow before afternoon lessons," said Xinia. She and Nell hurried their lunch and ran round to the stables to fit a horse hug in before they were due at the Summer Dojo.

Chapter 14

In the afternoon, it was time for another martial arts lesson with Sensei Goodwin. "Good afternoon!" he said. "I hope you didn't have too heavy a lunch!"

The students all lined up and exchanged bows with him as they wondered what he had in mind for them today.

"Today we are going to learn about trips and throws," announced Sensei Goodwin. "Now, you have just had lunch, so we will start this slowly. You can save the breakfalls and the throwing each other around for later when your sandwiches have gone down. I don't want anyone being sick and making a mess on my mat!"

The students giggled. This sounded fun, and the idea of being sick on the mat rather amused some of the boys.

Sensei Goodwin then went on to demonstrate various trip and throw techniques. He selected Charlie as his uke.

Charlie grinned and stepped forward eagerly, always keen to get involved and have a go at things. He was somewhat relieved when the Sensei took his balance without throwing him to the floor. Instead, he hung suspended on his way to the ground by his arm.

Sensei Goodwin lowered him there slowly. "See? You can practise trips without knocking your partner down hard. Give it a go!"

The students worked in pairs, copying the technique they had just seen. They took the arm of their attacker, stepped a foot behind him and pushed him gently off balance so that he would have fallen to the ground if his arm wasn't being held steady. They could see how this would be a very effective way of putting an attacker on his back. Yet they were able to practise it gently and without any danger to themselves or their lunch.

After a lot of practice and swapping partners to test the technique on different sized people, Sensei Goodwin moved on to throws. "Throws have many uses," he said. "Particularly if you are dealing with a lot of attackers at once, you want to be able to move those attackers away from you quickly and in a way that will slow them down. It is also rather nice that you can do this without necessarily really hurting them. You always have to be aware that throwing someone onto a hard surface can do a lot of damage. It can even kill them if they hit their head. Some people have very delicate heads and don't even know it.

But, in general, throwing someone is less harmful than something like a direct strike to the head. With all these techniques, you have to know the possible outcomes. When you do it on the mat, it is safe. But if you were to do this on hard ground, it would be very dangerous."

With his safety talk over, Sensei Goodwin started teaching them some throws. "Let's start the throws with some static ones. That means we start the techniques with everyone standing still. Later on, we will move onto how to throw someone who is running at you. That bit's fun! But it is best we start with the fundamentals. A house is built on its foundations!"

Sensei Goodwin taught them to do some variations on static throws. They learned to step with their back to their attacker, put their arm around his waist, around his shoulders or under his armpit, then swing their attacker over the side of their hips. "Don't try and throw him over your shoulder," said Sensei Goodwin. "You are too small for that, and when you get to my age, it will hurt your back for no good reason!"

The students laughed. They couldn't imagine being as old as Sensei Goodwin. He was surely as old as the stars! They practised what he taught them diligently, still being careful to simply take their attackers balance rather than slam them into the mat.

After an hour or so of practising trips and throws, Sensei Goodwin decided that everyone's lunches had gone down and it was time for a bit more action. "Do you remember learning to step around so that you take yourself off the line of attack? Do you remember when I did the demonstration with the boulder that ran down the hill at me? Do you remember how I stepped around, out of the path of the boulder so I could tap it from behind and send it on its way?"

The students all nodded eagerly. "That was brilliant!" cried Charlie, totally immersed in the dramatic memory of the boulder thundering down the slope to Sensei Goodwin and watching him spin around behind the boulder which then smashed into a wall.

"Well, we are going to do something similar now – except the boulder will be your attacker and no-one is going to smash into any walls!"

The students grinned. This was exciting!

"Let's make sure you remember your breakfalls and rolls

first. Line up and I want you to run at me one at a time. Raise your right arm and try and chop me on the head as you run in. You will play the part of the boulder. I will then move out of your path and project you to the ground. Don't worry; we will start this gently so you can get the hang of it."

Mark led the line of attackers. He ran at Sensei Goodwin, raised his arm and attempted to chop at his head. The next thing he knew, he was flying across the mat in a forward roll, wondering how he got there. Charlie was next. Mark was just getting to his feet when he saw Charlie flying across the mat after him. Then Xinia, Lucy and each of the other students. They all got to their feet, feeling a bit disorientated and bemused. They had undoubtedly experienced the technique but had no idea what had happened.

Sensei Goodwin roared with laughter. "You poor young warriors! I'm sorry, that must have been rather surprising for you. But no-one is hurt though, are they?"

The students shook their arms and legs, checking everything was fine, and no damage had been done. "We are okay, Sensei," said Mark. Everyone nodded and agreed.

"Would you show us that more slowly please, Sensei?" asked Lucy, who was keen to learn how to do this.

"Of course!" said Sensei Goodwin with a smile. "Since you asked, you can be the uke."

Lucy looked doubtful. She had wanted to watch Sensei Goodwin do the technique on someone else so she could see how he did it. Sensei Goodwin had been teaching for enough decades to know precisely what was going through her mind. "Being a uke is a wonderful way to learn a technique. You learn by receiving the technique. But don't worry, you will be able to watch it too, when I demonstrate again on someone else. Mark looks keen to try it again!"

Lucy went to the end of the mat and then ran at Sensei Goodwin and went to chop his head with her arm. This time, he slowed the technique right down. The students watched carefully as he stepped off the line of her attack and with the lightest of touch to her attacking arm to redirect her ultimate direction, he guided her on her way onwards and to the ground. She fell into an easy forward roll after appearing to trip over thin air. Lucy had been paying close attention to everything that happened to her body through this. She tried to record it like a movie in her mind so she could play it over and over later. This was reinforced when she then saw Sensei Goodwin repeat the technique on Mark.

"I think I have it, Sensei," said Lucy.

"Wonderful!" exclaimed Sensei Goodwin. "Then let's see you demonstrate it on one of your friends. Gina! Step forward please and be uke for Lucy.

Lucy took up her position and awaited the incoming attack from Gina. As Gina ran towards her, Lucy's supernatural ability to see energy as light kicked in. She saw Gina as a thousand points of light, streaking towards her. Lucy stepped around, as she had seen Sensei Goodwin do and her hands gently connected with Gina's arm as she moved on her arc. Lucy saw the pinpoints of light streak from where Gina had started, and forwards to where she had projected her and then saw them curl around and fade away as Gina rolled and came to a stop.

"Wow!" said Lucy, who had not been expecting this. "I saw...well, I saw..." She trailed off, not wanting to describe what she saw because she knew it wasn't normal and that she wouldn't be understood. But she was glowing with excitement at this new experience. In fact, she was glowing with ki. The technique had stirred up a whirlwind of energy within her. Xinia saw it and smiled gently. She was the only other one of the students who shared Lucy's second form of sight.

"I know what you saw," said Sensei Goodwin to her quietly. "It is good. Treasure it. It is a gift like no other. In time, it will be central to your martial art. For now, you must learn to work with it and appreciate it.

"Now!" Sensei Goodwin addressed the whole class, "let's all practise this in partners. Be very careful not to throw your partners into each other. So let's start slowly and build up."

Before long, the dojo was a mass of swirling and tumbling as the students ran at each other and were projected around the dojo. The students all had a wonderful time and were sorry when the lesson finally came to an end, and it was time for dinner.

Chapter 15

The students arrived at the Summer Dojo the next morning, ready for their lesson with Sensei Silver. He was waiting for them at precisely nine o'clock and raised an eyebrow when a couple of them dashed into line, nearly late.

"Today we are going to go for a little walk into the forest," he said, with his usual air of semi-menace. The students always felt a bit uncomfortable around him. He had never done or said anything particularly terrible, but he still managed to give the impression that he actually might. Whereas Sensei Goodwin joked a lot with them and Sensei Tanaka found amusement in almost everything he encountered, Sensei Silver appeared entirely humourless. He had the quiet threat of a prowling panther. The students were cautious around him, very keen to avoid making him angry. He was scary enough when he wasn't angry!

Still, a walk in the woods sounded nice – and innocent enough. The students all followed along behind him as he led them into the forest. He said nothing and they thought it best to stay quiet too.

After a while, Charlie went to say something, but Mark

nudged him and shook his head. Charlie understood and put his finger on his lip, which then made him want to giggle.

Sensei Silver stopped, turned around and fixed a level, cool gaze on Charlie, whose urge to giggle evaporated instantly. Sensei Silver looked at him a second longer. But it was one of those seconds that felt like minutes and certainly had the desired effect on Charlie. Then he turned and led the students on into the forest.

They arrived in a clearing in the forest, at the bottom of a long and quite steep hill. "Welcome to the Dead Oak Dojo," said Sensei Silver. "It is so named because of the expanse of dead oak trees over there."

He gestured to an area to the left of the clearing, the other side of a narrow river, where there must have been about a hundred oak trees which were completely devoid of life. They were just tall, grey looking trees with broken branches and no leaves. The entire area looked like a tree graveyard.

"And straight ahead is Botheration Hill," he said with a slightly sadistic smile. "The reason for that will become more obvious as the morning progresses."

The students didn't like the sound of that. His smile held the promise of a less than pleasant morning. They knew Sensei Silver enough by now to know that, if he was smiling, it wasn't something they were going to be smiling about.

"Do you remember the techniques you have been taught?" he asked with deceptive innocence.

"Yes, Sensei," the students all chorused.

He laughed. "Let's see, shall we? Let's start with simple windscreen wiper blocking. Get into pairs and show me what you can do."

The students heaved a sigh of relief. They knew how to do this, and they knew they were good at it. They formed up in pairs and went through the blocking sequence – upper left, upper right, lower left, lower right, their arms moving like the windscreen wipers of a car as they blocked a sequence of incoming punches: roundhouse from left, roundhouse from right, uppercut from left, uppercut from right. They had done this a hundred times in the Summer Dojo and felt they knew it well.

"Stop!" snapped Sensei Silver. "Now run up Botheration

Hill, touch the large Beech tree at the top, then run back here and do your blocking exercise again."

The students set off at a fast run, competing with each other to reach the top of the hill first. It was a close-run race. David touched it first, followed by Gina, then Mark and the others followed. Running downhill was easier than running up it, but they were still puffing and out of breath when they reached the bottom.

"Blocking! Now!" demanded Sensei Silver, not wanting them to have any recovery time before doing the exercise.

The students found their pairs quickly and got on with the exercise. To their surprise, they found it harder and found they were making mistakes.

"Not so easy now, is it?" said Sensei Silver. "Now do your block and punch. Three times each. Then run up the hill to the Beech tree again and run back and do the same exercise."

The students did as they were told. It was getting more challenging now, though. They were getting out of breath, and they ran up the hill slower this time. "Faster!" came the command from the bottom of the hill. They all picked up their pace, ran up to the Beech tree and headed back.

This time, when they did their block and punch exercise, they found they were getting confused, blocking with the wrong hand and therefore missing the incoming roundhouse punch from their partner. Some ended up punching their partner a bit too hard in their chest and winding them. They knew they were only meant to tap lightly in training, but now they were tired and out of breath, they were making mistakes.

"Up the hill again!" called Sensei Silver.

Up the hill they all ran again. This time, they had stopped competing. They were all just trying to get through the lesson.

Sensei Silver kept running them up the hill and getting them to do simple exercises when they returned. Each time, the students found that they couldn't do the simple exercises that they normally could manage without any difficulty. Eventually, when the students were ready to drop, Sensei Silver called "Enough!"

They all wanted to drop to the floor, but Sensei Silver wouldn't let them.

"No! Get up! You can't push your heart that hard and then just lay down. You have to bring it down slowly. So I want you to walk it off. Walk around this forest dojo in a big circle until your heart has slowed down."

Once he was satisfied that their heart rates had returned to normal, he let them sit down. Many of them laid out flat on the forest floor, staring up at the network of tree branches above them. He stood back and watched them, giving them a few minutes to relax before he said what he intended to them.

"Today, you learned an important lesson. You learned that it becomes hard to do techniques that you think you know well once your heart is racing. It is one thing to learn and practise techniques in the calm of a dojo, but once you are in battle conditions, it is a very different matter. You find you cannot do the things you think you can do."

He walked around the forest clearing, delivering his lecture and making sure that the students were paying attention. He had already made his point, of course, but this was his opportunity to explain it to them.

"So what do you do? Well, there are several elements to this solution. Firstly, you must train your muscle memory so that your conscious mind does not even have to get involved in the delivery of your technique. Mark, stand up."

Mark staggered to his feet. Sensei Silver put his hands to Mark's neck as if to strangle him, but didn't put any pressure on. "You were taught the Krav Maga Pluck?" he asked.

"Yes, Sensei," said Mark.

"Well, why aren't you doing it?" said Sensei Silver. "I don't ever want you to hesitate for a moment. There is no circumstance in which you should let someone strangle you. You don't have to think about it. The second their hands close around your throat, you pluck them away. Do it!"

Mark smartly plucked Sensei Silver's hands away from his throat.

"Better!" said Sensei Silver. "Sit down."

"So you must practise this technique a thousand times. You must drill it into your brain so hard that it becomes a part of your brain, and you will then do it as a reflex action. Until you have programmed your reflex response, you will find it hard to do this technique under battle conditions. Would you like to test that theory?" he asked wickedly.

"No, Sensei! Please!" all the students groaned at the thought of having to run up the hill again.

"I know. You think me very cruel. One day you will thank me for this lesson. One day you will find yourself in fight or battle conditions. You will find that your heart races, your hands shake, your legs wobble. Your mouth will go dry, and your vision will narrow to a restricted tunnel. Even your hearing will become tunnel-like. You might feel sick. Your thinking brain will be confused and terrified. At that moment, you will need two things – firstly, you will need all your techniques to be automatic reflex actions, because goodness knows your mind will not be capable of directing them. And secondly, you will want to have the ability to calm yourself so you don't feel all those horrible things.

"At this stage in your training, it is unlikely that you will be able to calm yourself in battle conditions. That is an ability you will train for later in your martial arts career. Some warriors never develop it, in fact. But what you can do at this stage is to train your muscle memory and reflex actions through a lot of practice. You may think that your Senseis are cruel and demanding when they make you practise again and again, long after you think you have learned a technique. But they are training your automatic response through repetition. You should aim to learn every technique so well you can do it with your eyes shut and under the harshest of battle conditions."

With this final advice, he gestured to them to follow and led them back through the forest to the Academy. As they were walking back, Charlie whispered to Mark, "Now, was that reasonable?" They both chuckled under their breath. Sensei Silver smiled to himself as he walked on ahead.

Chapter 16

The first week back at the Academy drew to a close and, at the weekend, the older students returned from their summer holiday for the next school year. They showed no interest in the new first-years, though.

Even the new second-years now considered themselves too far above the first-years to give them any attention. Mark and his friends were interested to see them. Each of them imagined that they would become like these older students in the years to come. It was interesting to see their future laid out before their eyes.

When the new week started, the school routine changed. Now that the holidays were over, the martial arts, ninjas skills, horsemanship and bodyguarding lessons had to share time on the schedule with more normal school lessons.

"We can't have you growing up experts in martial arts but ignorant of everything else, can we?" observed Professor Ballard. "You must have a well-rounded education. But because we have small classes, a very well designed curriculum and intensive use of time, you will find that you will eventually leave here with an excellent education to rival that provided in any other school. And, of course, you will have become highly trained warriors with some particular skills that will prepare you for careers as elite operatives."

The school day started at half-past seven in the morning. The entire school gathered on the grass in front of the main building for Tai Chi. Then there was breakfast at eight o'clock and first lesson at nine o'clock. The morning lessons were martial arts, ninja skills and horsemanship.

After lunch, there were a couple of hours of ordinary education, which were taught by teachers they hadn't met before. This block of two hours was typically spent on a single subject and involved special projects and intensive exercises designed to completely immerse the students in that subject.

At three o'clock, there was a half-hour break where the students could go for drinks and snacks. Then at half-past three in the afternoon, there were more lessons in martial arts, ninja skills and horsemanship.

The students were delighted to be allowed to move on from conducting their horsemanship lessons on fences and wooden horses to real horses. They learned the basics of horse care and riding. Throughout this, Carlotta stayed to one side and watched. She actually knew how to ride very well. She had been a keen rider before her mother's accident and had been taught very well. But she hadn't ridden since that terrible day and was very keen not to ride ever again. The mere sight of a horse put her on edge. She hoped that if she just watched the others in their lessons, she might gradually stop panicking at the sight of a horse.

Carlotta very soon got used to the idea of being at a school. Although she hadn't been to school before coming to the Academy, she found it suited her very well. The other students made her very welcome, and all had sworn to keep her safe. So she wasn't left alone for a moment. There were always at least a couple of other students with her.

Carlotta had often felt lonely in her previous life. With no brothers or sisters and no school friends, she had often felt very alone and bored. She had developed a rather extreme fashion sense in order to tell people to stay away. But the truth was that she actually wanted company. She wanted friends. She wanted people to be with, to talk to, to do things with. Now she was at the Academy, Carlotta found that she had all these things. She began to think it was a shame that she would have to go back to living on her own after this had passed, with just governesses and tutors for education and company.

Mark and Charlie were very excited to have the opportunity to be bodyguards. They often sent Lucy and Xinia off so they could have their go at bodyguarding Carlotta. "It's our turn now!" they would say. "We have to practise!"

The girls let them take their turn. There was no point arguing with the boys when they were on a mission. Other times, all the students would practise forming up the bodyguarding box as Sergeant Yeald had taught them and walking Carlotta around the grounds of the Academy. Sergeant Yeald was usually not far away. He watched with amusement as they practised their exercise, pleased that they had taken their job so much to heart.

And so the days became weeks and the weeks became months. Before long it was the end of November and then the start of December. All of the students were very happy at the Academy and were doing well in all their studies. They began to look forward to Christmas, which was just weeks away now.

Chapter 17

Meanwhile, at the Shadowlands School of Ninjas, the term had unfolded also. Pandora had more or less got used to the harsh routine. If the truth be known, she regretted getting herself thrown out of the Academy, but she would never admit it. Eaten up by anger and jealousy, which was directed at both the Academy and her sister Xinia, Pandora committed herself to training hard. She intended to become the best Ninja that Shadowlands had ever seen.

Instructor Jack Adams continued to drill them with constant sadism, his cruelty and determination relentless. He only seemed to be happy when the students were struggling and suffering. When they grazed their hands doing push-ups on the hard ground of the training yard, he would yell, "I want blood! Don't you stop! I want blood!" He would make the students continue with their push-ups until every student had bleeding hands. Then he would run them to the beach and make them plunge their suffering hands into cold, salty water which stung them as much as it cleaned them.

Instructor Adams was a great believer in training for the harshest of realities. Although his students were only just young teenagers, he drilled them like adult soldiers. He showed them no mercy and punished them if they showed the slightest mercy to each other. For some students, it was almost unendurable. For Pandora, it was an environment of darkness that matched the blackness of her own soul. She could not bear weakness in others and had no difficulty dishing out pain to her fellow students when Instructor Adams made them fight each other.

Their days may have been hard, but they were far from boring. Pandora was easily bored and had an extremely short attention span. She craved new experiences and change of activity all the time. The only thing she found unendurable was having to do the same thing for any lengthy period. Fortunately for her, any activity only lasted as long as it amused Instructor Adams.

There were fighting lessons, fitness training sessions and transport lessons where they learned to ride mountain bikes, motorbikes and horses. They were taught some of the history of the Ninjas and learned only so much of their ways that Shadowlands thought useful. There was regular education too. This was taught by other teachers in the Nissen hut classrooms.

The subjects were taught in a regimented and high-pressure way, with punishments for poor performance. Sometimes the penalties were things like push-ups or runs around the training camp. Other times, the punishments were designed to humiliate the students, such as sitting in the corner with a dustbin on their head. When Pandora was punished this way on one occasion for doing badly in a test, she was utterly outraged. "You can't do this to me! It's against the law!" she hissed. "What law? And who is going to enforce that?" came the reply from the strict instructor.

And so Pandora and her fellow students gradually developed as fighters and as operatives and were educated in subjects that they would need when they later went out into the world as Shadowlands agents. Pandora discovered that she had a talent for languages. She found that she could pick them up very easily. She started with French and German and very soon started learning Chinese and Japanese. The Shadowlands staff encouraged this. A talent for languages was a very useful ability for a Ninja and future Shadowlands operative. It would come in very handy when she went out into the world one day to do their work.

The term rolled on and headed towards December. Around this time, they were summoned to a special assembly where they were addressed by the headmaster of

Shadowlands. He hadn't bothered talking to them before now. Presumably, they were beneath his notice as new recruits. But now he had something to say to them.

He was a medium height man with greying hair and glasses. He looked unremarkable in every way. He looked like a bank clerk or something really boring. He certainly did not look like the headmaster of a Ninja school. He wore an ordinary suit, not particularly smart and not scruffy either. The students stared at him in amazement. They couldn't believe that this extraordinary place was being run by someone who looked so incredibly ordinary.

Pandora looked him straight in the eyes. She recognised something in him that she knew was in her – a heart as black as coal and a mind as cool as snow. She smiled. This man was truly a Ninja – his disguise would have fooled everyone. But it wouldn't fool someone who was made of the same stuff. Or rather, made with the same things missing.

He smiled. It was a deeply insincere smile. Most of the students were fooled by it. Pandora wasn't. She used that smile herself too. It was simply a device to disarm one's victims.

"I will come straight to the point," he said. "I have a little mission for you. This is your chance to show me what you can do and to show that you are worthy of your place at Shadowlands."

The students looked excited. This sounded interesting! They also welcomed the idea of a change of routine. Being worked to exhaustion every day was getting increasingly unpleasant. Perhaps this would be fun?

"You will all be aware by now of a rival school called The Academy."

There were nods and "Yes, Sir" coming from the students. Pandora had told them all about this terrible place that had been so unfair to her and how her wicked sister went there and took her place. They thought it sounded perfectly frightful.

"Well, it has come to our attention that the Academy is sheltering the daughter of a politician. That politician is a great risk to our country, and everything Shadowlands has been working for all these years. Do you know why?"

"No, Sir," they all replied, genuinely unaware of all this. If the truth were known, they weren't very interested in politics and didn't understand it either. But the headmaster was obviously going to tell them, whether they liked it or not.

"Her father is a man called Norman Fairweather. He has a subversive idea to introduce a law that ensures everyone has the freedom to say whatever they like. So that would mean that people could say awful things and no-one could stop them. Wouldn't that be terrible?"

The headmaster's tone of voice certainly conveyed the idea that this would be terrible. The students didn't really understand what he was talking about, but they nodded and agreed with him.

"You may realise by now that this Shadowlands Ninja School is part of a much larger organisation, an organisation committed to leading this country and the World into a bright future. Great plans have been made, and a lot of work has been done to bring society in line with these plans, both here and in other countries. We have operatives at every level of government and public life, everywhere you can imagine. We are united in our common purpose to lead society forward in an organised and structured way. Only through this new world order can all of society reach its full potential."

As he worked towards the end of this little speech, he appeared to grow beyond his weedy bank clerk appearance. He may look very average, but when he spoke, he was able to lead the mind of his listeners, to enthuse them with his message and leave them wanting to jump to their feet and roar their support.

The students were stunned. None of them had ever heard someone speak like this. They didn't quite see how everything fitted together, but they felt sure now that they were part of something significant. They were ready to do anything he asked them to - all perhaps, except Pandora. She saw through this man. She could see how he manipulated the students with his grand speech. She didn't have the same feelings that other students did. There was nothing in her that could get stirred up. She found that she never had the same kind of feelings as ordinary people. All she ever seemed to feel was anger or boredom. When she wasn't feeling either of those things, she was either in a neutral frame of mind or had the canny observation of a cat.

Right now, she was feeling like a cat. She watched, she heard, she analysed, and she knew what she was dealing with. She knew that he was trying to control the students and, judging by their rapt attention and shining eyes, he was achieving it. Pandora was clever enough to know that it was best to hide the fact she was different to others. So she looked at the girl next to her and made a point of copying her expressions. The headmaster didn't notice.

Now that he had their attention, he went on to outline what it was he wanted them to do. He told them that they were to launch an attack on The Academy and kidnap the politician's daughter. He explained that this was essential to preventing the politician from bringing down society with his Freedom of Speech bill.

"We can't stop this politician any other way. We can't pay him to stop. We can't threaten him to make him stop. But we can take his daughter. That should make him stop," explained the headmaster.

Chapter 18

It was a Saturday night, and the students at the Academy had enjoyed a delicious dinner followed by a movie, projected on a large screen in their common room. It had been about fantastic martial artists fighting to protect their Dojo in Japan. As they went up the stairs to bed afterwards, they were playing at being Samurai and challenging each other to sword fights with imaginary swords. There was much laughter and jollity.

When they got to their corridors, they all went off into their shared rooms with friendly calls of "Goodnight!"

Carlotta went into the room she shared with Xinia and Lucy. "That was a nice evening," she said. "I haven't seen a film like that before. I can see why you all want to become warriors when you grow up." Privately, she thought, *I might like that too.*

The Academy routine kept them very busy, and they had grown to value their sleep time. As Sensei Goodwin had told them, a martial artist needs their sleep because that is when their body recovers from their training and their mind processes all it had learned. So they looked on it as a special and enjoyable ritual. They knew that they would wake up the next day a little better than they had the day before, their muscles developed, and their minds enhanced with new training. The girls got themselves to bed and fell asleep soon after their heads hit the pillow.

Their sleep was to be interrupted, though. Around midnight, Mark and Charlie came into their room and shook them awake. "Ssshhhh!" they said to each of them. "What's up, Mark?" asked Xinia.

"Something is happening. Ninjas are attacking the Academy! We have to get Carlotta to safety," whispered Mark.

"Am I not safe here?" asked Carlotta quietly.

"This is the first place they will look," said Charlie. "And if they don't find you in these first-year bedrooms, they will search the whole building until they find you."

"They won't expect her to be at the stables though," pointed out Xinia. "And if they come into this room and see me, they will think I am Carlotta. That's why we made ourselves look alike. So you boys take Carlotta to the stables, and I will wait here with Lucy and fool them as a decoy."

"But if they think you are Carlotta, they will take you instead," pointed out Mark.

"We are bodyguards. This is part of the risk we took on when we agreed to guard Carlotta. Besides which, I reckon they will just let me go when they realise they have taken the wrong girl," replied Xinia.

"You are very brave," said Charlie admiringly. "It's quite a risk."

"I will be fine. Now get Carlotta to safety before it is too late!" ordered Xinia, sounding braver than she felt. She knew she was taking a big chance, but she knew how important it was that Carlotta didn't get taken. This was about more than protecting their friend. It was also about protecting their country and its freedoms.

So the boys whisked Carlotta away. There were ninjas everywhere, but they had the advantage of knowing the building and grounds better than the invaders. As they sneaked across the landing overlooking the entrance hall, they looked down and saw a firework display of streaking gold light.

In the middle of the entrance hall was the White Ninja that

Mark had spied on one night during the selection course. He hadn't seen the White Ninja since that strange night, but now it was here, swirling around, dispatching ninjas to all corners of the hall. Long white hair streaked in the air, appearing to crackle with electricity as the White Ninja spun and flew. Although the ninjas were being thrown around the hallway, the White Ninja wasn't hurting them. The ninjas were just being kept busy. The White Ninja had a long staff which glowed both gold and blinding white light as it moved.

Mark and Charlie wished they could stay and watch the incredible sight for longer. But they knew their job was to get Carlotta to safety. So they led her away down the back corridors to the door at the back of the building. They saw a figure out there and hesitated a moment. Then they heard a low whicker from nearby and recognised the outline of TigerLily against the moonlit sky.

"Mr Liu?" asked Mark quietly.

"Yes," he confirmed. "Have you got Carlotta?"

"Yes, we are going to take her to the stables," said Charlie.

"No, you should get her off the grounds entirely," said Mr

Liu. "She isn't safe here. You must take her into the forest. You have learned to navigate through the forest in the dark during your Ninja Skills lessons, haven't you?"

"Yes, Sir," said Mark.

"Take her to the Green Hornet Dojo. I will deal with any attackers and join you there shortly," he said. "Can you manage that?"

"Of course!" whispered Mark and Charlie together, grinning at each other. This was going to be exciting! They were keen to put their Ninja skills to the test.

"Move quickly and with as much stealth as you can!" warned Mr Liu. "Go!"

The boys set off quickly with Carlotta, blending around buildings, watching to make sure they didn't present silhouettes against the moonlit sky. As they moved away from the main building and down the path towards the Summer Dojo which led on into the forest, Mark looked back. He saw Mr Liu, standing in the middle of a circle, surrounded by ninjas and looking extremely still and peaceful. Mark hesitated a moment, wondering whether they should go back and help him. He didn't want Mr Liu getting hurt. He needn't have worried, though.

As the circle of ninjas moved in, determined to eliminate him and get access to the back door of the school, Mr Liu went into action. He flowed around them like water, evading every attack, causing the ninjas to crash into each other. It seemed that Mr Liu didn't actually touch anyone. The ninjas just kept missing him and falling over whilst Mr Liu appeared to be almost dancing, moving with a beautiful fluidity and quiet power.

Again, Mark wanted to stay and watch. He had never seen fighting like this - if it could be called fighting even. It all seemed so peaceful and gentle, yet the attacking ninjas were tumbling around like nine pins.

"Mark!" Charlie hissed. "We have to get her away!"

"Yes, of course," said Mark. "Let's go!"

The boys made their way down the path and out into the forest with Carlotta. It was very dark inside the woods, but their training served them well. It wasn't long before they reached the large oak tree that marked the Green Hornet Dojo. But, being midnight, Mr Woodpecker was asleep and was not able to confirm their location. They could hear the river nearby. They were definitely at the right spot. They all sat down, leaning against the big tree for support and cover. They waited.

It wasn't long before Mr Liu and TigerLily joined them. He appeared completely unharmed. "Are you okay?" asked Mark, "that was a lot of ninjas that attacked you."

"I am fine thank you. Fortunately, they just kept falling over."

Mark giggled. He had seen how that had played out. "You were incredible!" he said. "I saw everything. How did you learn to fight like that? I want to learn too!"

Mr Liu gave a little chuckle. "I wasn't fighting, I was just having a little dance."

"A dance in which a dozen ninjas kept falling over themselves?" asked Mark.

"Quite so!" said Mr Liu with a grin. "It's a very useful kind of dance. Now, let's get you all to safety. You aren't safe here; there could be ninjas in the woods."

He led them across a small wooden bridge over the river, turned left and took them onto an area of the forest they hadn't been to before.

"Where are we going?" asked Charlie.

"We are going to the Secret Island," said Mr Liu. "They won't find you there. It is almost impossible to find unless you really know the way."

He took them along the bank of the river, then through a clearing in the bracken that had five exit paths. He selected the second of the paths and took them up a long ridge of raised ground, down the other side and onto a new path. Only the forest ponies knew this path. Humans rarely passed this way. When they did, it was as if this part of the forest had been designed to have no navigation points of reference. Charlie asked Mr Liu if they should lay some Waymarks.

"No. Never mark this area. It must always remain secret. You never know when you will need that secrecy, like tonight."

"But how will we get home?" asked Charlie.

"TigerLily will take you," assured Mr Liu.

"Won't you be staying with us?" asked Mark.

"No, I have to get back and help out at the school," he replied. "But don't worry, you couldn't be safer than on the Secret Island. No-one will find you there."

They walked on a little longer and then stopped. To their left was a thin arch formed by the bending and intertwining of young trees. It was almost invisible, but once you knew what you were looking for, it was quite clearly an entrance and a lovely one at that.

"This is the entrance to the Secret Island. It can only be seen from a certain angle and only by those who have an eye for such beauty," said Mr Liu. "It cannot be seen by those of dark and evil heart."

He led them through the archway. It led to an island of forest, caught between two rivers which joined at the far end. It was technically a peninsula in that it was not entirely cut off from land by water. But the hidden archway cut this place off from the mainland just as effectively as a few more feet of river would have done.

There was an extraordinary atmosphere on the Secret Island. Although it was night time, it was bathed in moonlight, which streamed through the openings in the trees and lit the entire island. Glowworms peppered the ground and illuminated the bracken. There were also various plants that emitted bioluminescence of various colours. The island looked completely magical with this subtle light display.

"Why are there so many special plants and bugs here?" asked Carlotta, wide-eyed with amazement. She had never seen anything so beautiful.

"Because humans rarely come here. These glowworms only thrive where their habitat is undisturbed. So be very careful and respectful of their home whilst you are here please. Honour the sanctuary they are giving you."

Carlotta made a little bow to the glow worms. "Thank you, kind Sirs," she said.

Mr Liu chuckled. "Actually it is the females who glow. But they appreciate your thanks!

"Now, I really must get back to the Academy. Wait here until morning. TigerLily will stay with you and bring you back then."

With that, Mr Liu stroked TigerLily's magnificent neck, whispered something private in her ear and then vanished from the island in a few steps. Then they were alone. TigerLily found a comfortable looking patch amongst the bracken and laid down. Mark, Charlie and Carlotta huddled up and leant back against a large tree.

Mark and Charlie tried to stay awake and on guard, but it was so peaceful on the Secret Island, they were lulled to sleep by the trickling sounds of the river and the ethereal glow of the glow worms and glowing plants.

In the shadows, a dark figure watched them silently. The figure remained hidden and, as on so many other previous occasions, remained unnoticed by the students who now slept peacefully, safer than even they knew.

The next thing they knew, it was morning and Mark was being nudged awake by TigerLily. She was on her feet and standing over him. He giggled as the soft horse nose whiffled at his hair and cheek.

"We had better get back! They will be wondering what happened to us!" said Mark as he woke the other two.

Chapter 19

The students of Shadowlands School of Ninjas set off in trucks to launch an attack on the Academy, the mission briefing from Instructor Adams still ringing in their ears. They were to capture Carlotta Fairweather and take her back to Shadowlands.

Upon arrival, they split up. One group of them attacked the front of the building and another group attacked the back. Both of these sets of ninjas had met resistance. The ninjas who broke through the front of the building were accosted by a mysterious White Ninja who had flown around the entrance hall, sending them all to the corners of the hall with the slightest flick of a staff that glowed with blinding gold light.

The ninjas who had attacked the back of the building were met by an even stranger sentinel: a man who was dressed as a gardener but whose martial arts were so advanced, he barely had to touch his attackers to cause them to fall down. The ninjas had no idea what to make of this. They had anticipated resistance and had expected to win by virtue of their numbers. But a dozen of them had tried to attack this one man and had been sent flying with superhuman ease.

A third group of Shadowlands ninjas managed to gain entrance to the building through a side door at the end of a wing. Pandora had told them where to go if they were successful in getting through the back door. So it was easy for them to go up the back stairs, along the first-year dormitory corridor and to the two rooms there with girl's names on the door.

They were lucky. The first door that they opened had three beds in it, but only two names on the door. This was clearly where the Politician's daughter was being hidden.

Melanie, one of the older Shadowlands students, nudged one of her companions and whispered: "Look, the one in that bed matches the description!"

The companion, a slightly tubby lad called George, fished a crumpled photo out of his pocket. It was a newspaper photo of Carlotta, a couple of years ago before she had started putting bright colours in her hair. The two of them looked at the photo and then at the girl sleeping in the bed. They both had long dark hair. It was a good match. They had their target!

Melanie fished a black hood out of her backpack. Then they all held the sleeping girl still whilst Melanie pulled the hood over her head. The girl woke and wriggled and screamed.

In the other bed, another girl was woken by the screams. She was soon on her feet and fighting the intruders with everything she had. But there were too many of them. The gang of ninjas overcame her. They wrestled her to the ground and tied her hands to her bedpost.

Her screams of fury followed them as they hurried their captive down the corridor, down the back stairs and out the back door. They didn't care, though. They had achieved their objective. They hurried their captive along, tripping and stumbling because she couldn't see through the dark hood. Once they got out of the Academy grounds, they bundled her into a truck with them. Then, delighted with the success of their first really important mission, they sang songs of victory all the way back to Shadowlands. The rest of the Shadowlands students followed behind in the second truck, having withdrawn from the building when the kidnappers had whistled to them to let them know that they had the target.

Instructor Jack Adams was waiting for them back at Shadowlands, pacing impatiently. When he saw the trucks approach and flash their lights to let him know the mission was successful, he smiled. Oh yes! He had proven his worth as an instructor this time. He had taken a bunch of raw recruits and turned them into a fighting force capable of executing a mission of great importance! The headmaster would be impressed with him. Perhaps he would give him a bit of respect after this!

He waved the trucks to park up by the Nissen huts where they would be holding their captive initially. The trucks parked up and the students piled out, dragging their captive with them, her head still covered with the black hood. Instructor Adams smiled. He could see her long dark hair flowing from under the hood. His students had done it! He was almost proud of them.

"Come with me!" he said. "Bring the girl."

"You boy – go and fetch the headmaster from his office. He will want to see this," he pointed at one of the students and sent him off to do his bidding. It was the middle of the night now, but the headmaster would have been waiting up to see the result of the mission, just as Instructor Adams had.

The students filed into the Nissen hut. Melanie and George marched their captive in, each holding one of her arms.

The captive was strangely silent. She had been ever since they had put her in the truck. Now they pushed her into a seat. Then they stood behind her, one at each shoulder, ready to pounce if she dared move. She didn't, though. She just sat perfectly still and said nothing.

Instructor Adams stood in front of the girl, his arms folded across his chest. He was waiting for the headmaster to appear before he unveiled his prize. The headmaster wouldn't want to miss that.

The door opened and in walked the headmaster, his weaselly eyes shining with anticipation and satisfaction. He knew that the powers above him would be very pleased with the outcome of this operation. They had the girl! Now they would be able to stop the indomitable Norman Fairweather MP from undoing all their work and ruining the country! This was a great moment indeed!

The headmaster smiled at the students. Well, it ought to have been a smile, but his was a face that simply wasn't quite capable of a smile. But the students had worked out by now that this was the form his features took when he was pleased. They took that as encouragement enough – or, at least, as much encouragement as they were ever going to get from him.

Instructor Adams grabbed the top of the black hood that covered the captive girl's head. "Headmaster, I have great pleasure in presenting to you the one and only Carlotta Fairweather!"

With a flourish, he pulled the hood off the girl's head and stood back, looking very pleased with himself. The students all peered at her with interest. The headmaster gave her a sadistic grimace. Instructor Adams noted that the girl looked just like the girl in the newspaper photo they had been given to help identify her.

There was a snort of laughter. It was Pandora. The headmaster had developed a dislike of this girl, who didn't seem to respond to him as the other students did. She didn't seem to fear him as they did, and when she looked at him, it was as if she could see right through him. She seemed to see what he truly was, and it didn't impress her as it ought to.

"Yes?" he snapped impatiently at Pandora, not even looking at her, such was his distaste for this girl. "Is there something about Carlotta Fairweather that amuses you, Pandora?" he asked with a tone of menace in his voice.

"That's not Carlotta! That's my sister Xinia!" laughed

Pandora.

Xinia smiled. Her plan had worked, and now she found it quite funny. It hadn't escaped her notice though that she was now in a dangerous position. She had been kidnapped, and she couldn't be sure that they would let her go.

The headmaster's face turned an interesting shade of pink and then purple as his anger bubbled up inside him. "They got the wrong girl?!" he spluttered at Instructor Adams, whose anger was simmering up too.

"So it would appear, Sir," said the instructor, far from amused.

"We will discuss this later," snapped the headmaster before spinning on his heel and marching out.

Instructor Adams turned to the students, rage shining from his eyes. They all took a sharp intake of breath and stepped back away from him. They knew how angry he got at the best of times. This was certainly not going to be the best of times. They prepared for the onslaught that followed.

"You stupid, stupid children!" he spat. "You had one job! How hard was it to go and grab one girl and bring her back here?"

Xinia sat back in her chair and enjoyed the tirade he then delivered. Her kidnappers hung their heads in shame, visibly shaken by the tornado of Instructor Adams' incandescent anger.

She had imagined it would last about ten minutes or so. But an hour later he was still ranting at them, lecturing them, forcing them to drop to the floor and do press-ups and sending batches of them out to run around the grounds. Although the students had already done a late-night mission, and it was now the early hours of the morning, he showed them no mercy and kept up a relentless stream of punishment. Xinia said nothing, though. She thought it best to stay quiet and escape his wrath. She was of no interest to him now, so it was best not to attract attention.

As the students were limping back into the hut after yet another punishment run, they saw a tall figure march through the gates of the training camp. The guards on the gate had shrunk back in fear from this man. He was dressed from head to foot in black, had long black hair and an air of extreme danger. He clearly meant business. A couple of the braver ninjas students ran towards this stranger to challenge him but skidded to a stop when he gave them a hard look. They backed off, realising almost too late that it would be a bad idea to attack.

He stood in the middle of the training yard and waited, with a quiet patience that felt lethal to the onlookers. Eventually, Instructor Adams emerged.

The man in black fixed him with a steady gaze and said quite simply "You have something of ours." He held out his hand, clearly waiting for it to be returned.

Instructor Adams assessed him in a moment. He had some idea of what he could be dealing with here, and it wasn't worth the fight. The man in black was obviously a warrior from the Academy. Judging by his fearless confidence, the way he held himself and the terror he induced in all he looked at, he was a force to be reckoned with - a very dangerous force.

Instructor Adams held the door to the Nissen hut wide open and addressed Xinia. "Your lift home has arrived."

Xinia wasted no time. She got to her feet and slipped out of the open door past Instructor Adams. She had never imagined the day she would be delighted to see Sensei Silver, but she found that this was that day. There he was, looking magnificently deadly and threatening. He had come for her. He had come to rescue her. She smiled and started running towards him. He shook his head very slightly. She instantly knew what he was telling her, what he was teaching her even at that moment. She dropped back to a determined walk, her shoulders back and head high. She wasn't going to show fear.

He turned and walked back out of the Shadowlands camp, with Xinia at his side. They said nothing. The Shadowlands students watched them go with respect and wonder. They had been quite affected by this interesting and terrifying stranger.

Waiting for them in the woods were two horses, one as black as the night and the other a glowing silver-white. "Rainbow!" exclaimed Xinia, running to her horse and flinging her arms around his neck to hug him.

Sensei Silver smiled and mounted his own horse. "You did well in there. We had better get you back to the Academy."

Xinia swung herself up onto Rainbow and rode steadily back through the forest with Sensei Silver. He didn't speak again. She was exhausted by now and was almost asleep by the time they returned. Rainbow knew he had the important job of getting his human back to safety, so he followed the big black horse and carried Xinia's half-asleep figure all the way home.

Chapter 20

Breakfast that morning was an extended affair. It was a Sunday morning, so there were no lessons scheduled for the day. After the events of the night before, the students were chattering with great excitement about all that had happened.

"Where did you get to?" David asked Mark. "We saw that Carlotta and Xinia were missing."

"Charlie and I took her away into the forest so the ninjas couldn't take her," said Mark.

"Didn't they follow you there?" asked David.

Mark, Charlie and Carlotta exchanged subtle glances. Whilst they were making their way home that morning, they had agreed that they wouldn't mention the Secret Island to anyone else. They reasoned that Mr Liu had shared it with them because of the extraordinary circumstances. But it was a very special place. It needed protection from too many visitors because of the extraordinary wildlife there. Besides which, it wouldn't stay secret if everyone knew about it!

"We found a quiet spot in the forest. They didn't come anywhere near us," said Mark. Fortunately, there was so much to talk about; it was easy to move on from that part of the story.

"What happened to you, Xinia?" asked Gina. "Are you okay?"

"Well, it was a bit scary at times," said Xinia. "They put a hood over my head, dragged me from my bed, out of the building and into a truck. They were singing in the trucks because they were so pleased with themselves. I could tell then that it was just young people like ourselves, so I wasn't so worried then. I didn't think they would do anything really terrible to me."

"They didn't hurt you?" checked Lucy.

"No. They were a bit rough, of course, but they didn't hurt me intentionally. I thought I might be in trouble though when they worked out that they had taken me instead of Carlotta. Their instructor went really mad! My sister Pandora was there. She thought it was all hilarious. That just made the instructor and headmaster angrier. They have a really mean instructor, and their headmaster is creepy. I tell you what – it made me appreciate everyone here!"

"How did you get away?" asked Mark, who was hearing all this for the first time.

"Oh, you should have seen it!" said Xinia. "Sensei Silver just marched into their camp and demanded they hand me over. He was utterly terrifying! The ninjas just shrunk away from him and let him pass. Then they just let me go. No one wanted to argue with him."

"I can imagine!" giggled Lucy.

"He was much scarier there than he is with us," said Xinia. "It was as if he had a large bubble of energy around him that they seemed to sort of bounce off."

"He got our Xinia back, so I think he is a hero!" said Lucy.

The students all agreed with this. It sounded like it was all rather dangerous and Xinia was lucky that he had turned up and got her out.

"Guess who he had brought with him to take me home?" said Xinia with a big smile. "Rainbow! He brought my horse for me. I was so glad to see Rainbow after all that had happened. I just got on him, and he brought me home."

"Aw! Lovely Rainbow!" said Lucy.

"Tell you what, we saw some amazing martial arts last night!" said Charlie. "Firstly, there was a strange warrior, all dressed in white and with long flowing white hair, fighting off all the ninjas in the hallway. Mark calls her the White Ninja, don't you Mark?"

Mark nodded enthusiastically. "Yes, I have seen the White Ninja before. I have never seen his or her face, though. I don't even know if it is a man or a woman. Whenever the White Ninja is training or fighting, it moves so fast you can't see."

"And the light!" exclaimed Charlie. "There was light shining all over the place. The White Ninja had a great staff that glowed with really bright light, and left trails of light in the air."

"The White Ninja must live here somewhere," said Mark. "Last time I saw it, it was in the hall on the other side of the entrance, opposite the Refectory. That room gets kept locked, but I looked through the keyhole at night, and there it was, flying around the room with that light staff streaming everywhere!"

"I tell you what else was amazing," said Charlie. "Mr Liu! He was unbelievable!"

133

"Oh yes! He was incredible! He took on a dozen ninjas outside the back door to give us time to take Carlotta away," Mark explained. "But the amazing thing was that he didn't seem to touch any of the attackers. It was like he was doing his Tai Chi, but a little faster. He just moved around in a kind of dance, a great big smile on his face, whilst his attackers kept falling over and bouncing into each other. I don't know what that martial art was, but I seriously want to learn it!"

"I expect they will teach us all these things in our time here," said Lucy, who had lived at the Academy for many years because her mother was the Academy Doctor. "The students all arrive here knowing nothing, like us. But they end up like the instructors. We will too."

They all looked at each other, imagining what they would all be like one day. It was an inspiring thought.

"I wonder if they will be back for me," said Carlotta, somewhat worried. "If they came for me last night, they will probably try again."

At that moment, Professor Ballard passed by and heard what Carlotta said. "You are right, young lady. But don't worry, we will make a plan to keep you safe. We are going to have to find a safe place to take you. Things are still going to be rather tricky until your father gets his Bill through Parliament. We have to keep you safe right up to Christmas, I'm afraid. I hope you do not mind your time with us too much, though."

Carlotta smiled at him. "No, Sir. I love it here!" He nodded at her in acknowledgement, pleased that she was happy at the Academy.

"Well done, everyone. You all did very well last night. Xinia, you were extremely brave. Thank you for what you did. I am glad we got you back with no harm done. Mark and Charlie, you did very well to get Carlotta away. You did exactly what we trained you to do, and it worked out very well.

"Now, if you will excuse me, I must meet with Sergeant Yeald and some of the other Senseis. We must work out what we are going to do next to keep you safe, Carlotta."

With that, he left and went to his meeting.

The students carried on with their leisurely breakfast, enjoying the homemade damson jam that Cook had put out with the toast as a special treat.

As breakfast came to an end, James and Malcolm whispered to each other.

"Are you thinking what I am thinking?" asked James.

"I bet I am!" replied Malcolm. "Shall we ask our Dad?"

"No, let's speak to Professor Ballard first before we bother him. It might not be what they want to do. If we mention it to him now, Mum will have the bedrooms all made up by lunchtime! You know how much they love having guests!"

James and Malcolm left the Refectory and headed off to Professor Ballard's office. They knocked and were called inside. As they opened the door, they saw Professor Ballard at his desk, Sergeant Yeald by the window and half a dozen Senseis around the room, some seated and others standing.

"Yes? Can we help you?" asked Professor Ballard.

"I think we might be able to help you, Sir," said James with a smile.

"Oh yes!" cried Malcolm. "You need somewhere safe to take Carlotta where those bad ninjas can't get her, don't you?"

136

"Well, yes, we do," admitted Professor Ballard. "That's what we were just considering, in fact."

"We could all go up to our parent's estate in Scotland!" suggested James. "Mum and Dad love having visitors. It is miles from anywhere, and it's a castle! There is room for everyone."

"Would you like us to ask our Dad?" asked James. "I am sure he will be keen to help."

Professor Ballard raised his eyebrows, considering the idea for a moment. He knew their father very well, of course. He had been a student at the Academy. He exchanged glances with Sergeant Yeald and the Senseis. There were a lot of nods from around the room.

"That's a brilliant suggestion. Thank you, boys," said Professor Ballard. "It is better I speak to him, though. There will be a lot to consider and discuss. Run along now, and I will let you know what is going to happen later on."

Once the boys left, the Senseis, Professor Ballard and Sergeant Yeald talked it over. All agreed that it was an excellent idea. They decided that Professor Ballard should call the boys father and see if it would be possible.

137

"How will we get them all up to Scotland?" asked Sensei Goodwin. "It's a long way, and I think we need to take the whole class in order to maintain lessons and keep a decent-sized guard around her."

"Oh, I have some contacts in the Navy. Excellent fellows. I am sure they will give us a lift in one of their larger helicopters," said Sergeant Yeald confidently. "If they can shift great troops of soldiers, I am sure they can manage a dozen teenagers!"

Chapter 21

There was great excitement amongst the students on their journey up to Scotland. Sergeant Yeald had been as good as his word and had managed to arrange a large military helicopter to transport them there. With their bags safely stowed in a large container, the students were all strapped securely into rather basic looking seats.

Nell wriggled on the sparsely padded seat. "I hope this isn't going to take very long. These seats are rather uncomfortable!"

"I already asked," said Mark. "It should be just over two hours - maybe faster as this is a big, powerful helicopter. It probably goes faster than civilian ones."

Lucy giggled. "I hope so! It doesn't look like there will be air hostesses bringing drinks and snacks around."

Charlie sighed, with fake drama to amuse everyone. "Such is the life of a great warrior!"

"I expect that's why they issued us with water bottles and snacks to go in our pockets," observed Xinia.

James and Malcolm settled back on their seats. They were

used to making this journey by air. "Really, it won't take long, and then we will all be in Scotland," said James.

"You are going to love it there!" said Malcolm. "If you thought the forest at the Academy was good, wait until you see the Scottish Highlands!"

"Indeed," said Sergeant Yeald, who was travelling with the students to maintain close protection for Carlotta. "Stags the size of horses! Views that go on forever. It is an excellent place and perfect for hiding Carlotta."

Carlotta looked a bit shy. " I am so sorry to take you all away from your school and drag you all the way up to Scotland!"

"It is our pleasure!" cried Mark. "We are really excited to get our first opportunity to go on a proper mission and learn how to bodyguard. You have done us all a great favour! I bet no other class at the Academy got to do what we are doing."

"Absolutely, dear boy!" said Sergeant Yeald. "This is a great opportunity for you all. There is so much to learn and no lovelier place to learn it!"

The students all agreed that great adventures and opportunities lay ahead. They chattered with excitement until the blades of the helicopter began to turn.

Sergeant Yeald waved his headset at them and raised his voice above the thudding of the blades. "You had better get your ear protectors on. I'm afraid helicopters get rather noisy!"

Mark and his friends put their ear protectors on, relieved to have the loud noise muffled. For the hours that followed, all they could do was smile and gesture to each other. Although the ride was bumpy and the noise was still droning through the ear protectors, they found themselves eventually dropping off to sleep.

The next thing they knew, Sergeant Yeald was tapping them on the shoulder. "Okay, you lot! Wake yourselves up! We are here!"

The students rubbed bleary eyes as the chopping of the helicopter blades slowed to a stop. Sergeant Yeald was right. They had landed.

A large ramp at the back of the helicopter dropped.

"Come on then everyone! Time to disembark!" ordered Sergeant Yeald.

The students fumbled with their safety harnesses, still somewhat sleepy. But they were soon free of them and following Sergeant Yeald out of the helicopter. As they were getting up to go out, Charlie grumbled, "I didn't get to eat my snacks!"

"That means you still have them left to eat now," pointed out Lucy.

Charlie cheered up and grinned at her.

Once they were out of the helicopter, the students were able to take stock of where they had landed. Even though they were now used to the splendour of the Academy, the scene before them took their breath away. Before them stood a tall castle. Behind it, they could see a large dark lake with ranges of snow-topped mountains beyond. They had landed on a large green in front of the castle, which lay amongst horse paddocks and forest on the edge of the large expanse of water.

"This is where you live?" Xinia turned to James and Malcolm in amazement.

"Home, sweet home!" replied Malcolm with a broad smile. He was justly proud of his family estate.

James was about to say something when the large wooden front doors of the castle swung wide and out came the welcoming party. Leading it was James and Malcolm's father, the Laird of Muckleben, followed by his wife and Senseis Goodwin and Tanaka. The Senseis had travelled up the day before to make some arrangements and so were here to welcome them now.

"Welcome! Welcome! You are all so very welcome!" exclaimed the Laird. "I am Doig Wallace of Muckleben, and this is my lady wife, Lady Norma." He put his arm around the beautiful woman at his side whose long red hair fell in cherry copper waves around her shoulders.

"Hello, everyone! You must be starving after your long journey! Come away inside and have some tea!" Lady Norma waved everyone towards the open front doors.

The tea she had arranged for them was sumptuous. The heavy, long wooden table in the Grand Dining Room was laden with every good thing that a young person might like and a lot they wouldn't have thought of. As Mark swept his glance along the big table, he was delighted to see all sorts of baked treats, including tea cakes, oat and blueberry scones, fudge, shortbread, coconut cake, apple pie and a fruited cake that he learned was a Dundee cake. It was all delicious and made the students feel very welcome.

"I'm not going to need those snacks for a bit!" observed Charlie.

"Oh, I am sure you will find room for them later," chuckled Mark.

"That's true!" said Charlie with a grin.

"I can't believe how beautiful your house is," said Xinia to James and Malcolm. "It's a real castle, isn't it?"

"Yes!" replied James. "It is called Kaey Castle – and that is Kaey Loch you saw behind it."

"Loch?" asked Lucy. "What's a Loch?"

"Well, it's a kind of Scottish lake," said Malcolm. "It's very big and very deep."

"Does it have a monster like Loch Ness?" asked Nell, her eyes wide at the thought.

"No one really knows," said Malcolm. "There are tales, of course, but that's all. It is certainly deep enough for a monster. It is said that it is as deep as a mountain in the middle!"

"Do you have many horses here?" asked Xinia. She was missing Rainbow already.

"Dozens!" said James, smiling. "Dad is a great horseman. Both my parents are horse mad. They take in horses that other people have hurt or abandoned. If a horse is in trouble in these parts, it always seems to end up here."

Xinia was impressed. These sounded like exceptionally lovely people. She couldn't wait to meet all the horses they had taken in.

Carlotta was less impressed. She had hoped to get away from horses when they came up to Scotland. But she knew she was in the safest place right now. The memory of the ninja attack on the Academy was still fresh in her mind. She dreaded to think what would have happened if they had managed to capture her. It didn't bear thinking about. What would they have done to her and what would they have made her father do? And what could that have done to the freedom of the whole country? She might be just a small girl, but she knew that she could be used to create tremendous harm to others. She resolved to trust her protectors and co-operate with what they had planned to keep her safe.

Chapter 22

After the meal, Sensei Goodwin told them that they could amuse themselves that afternoon – as long as they were good and respectful guests. He warned them that lessons would resume the following day, though.

The students all turned to James and Malcolm with expectant looks.

"The guided tour?" asked James.

"Yes, please," they all called.

"Well, let's start with your bedrooms," said Malcolm. "Grab your bags, and let's go and put them in your rooms before we go exploring."

The eight guests picked up their bags from where they had left them, lined up against the wall of the Grand Dining Room. They chased off after James and Malcolm as they took them to their rooms. They made their way up a large and ornate wooden staircase and then along winding corridors and up a stone stairwell.

"This is the North Turret," explained James. "We have rooms elsewhere in the castle, but we are going to bunk in

147

with the other boys on the second floor as we have to keep together to protect Carlotta. The girls have the room above."

He flung a studded wooden door open to reveal the boys' room. It was a large circular room with five beds arranged around the outside. Three windows in the stone wall flooded the room with light. "Please, choose your beds!" invited Malcolm.

Mark put his bag on the bed nearest the door, keen to claim the prime guard position. Charlie took the bed next to Mark's. David chose a bed facing the door, with a window behind it. James and Malcolm were happy to take the two beds that were left.

Whilst the boys were settling in, James took the girls up another flight of stairs to the room directly above the boys. "Make yourselves at home!" he invited and left them to choose their beds, calling over his shoulder. "Don't be long, there is a lot to show you this afternoon!"

The girls debated amongst themselves, trying to work out the best place to put Carlotta. In the end, they decided it was best that she was between Lucy and Xinia on the side of the room that the back of the door opened on to. Gina and Nell put themselves on the beds closest to the door as it opened. With this decided and their bags dropped on their selected beds, they climbed back down the steep stone stairwell to the boys' room to begin the guided tour.

James and Malcolm set off at quite a pace, leading them all over the castle, pointing out areas they should avoid for the sake of politeness, such as his parents' rooms and the staff quarters. They showed them a fantastic library with long cases of books that were arranged over three levels.

"Of course, you know where the important room is – the dining room!" laughed Malcolm. "But you will need to know where the Ballroom is, as that's where our classes will be held."

He led them back to the ground floor and to a pair of tall golden doors. He opened them and led them inside. It was dark at first until Malcolm drew back curtains that covered some very tall windows. As the light was let in, it illuminated a room almost entirely walled in gold and mirrors. Some of the students gasped. This was a magnificent room!

"Our parents like to hold grand parties sometimes!" laughed Malcolm.

Charlie and Gina linked hands and pretended to ballroom dance around the room as some of the others sang songs for them to dance to. Everyone fell about laughing.

"What's all this noise?" asked a voice behind them. It was Sensei Goodwin. The students stopped their messing around instantly and turned to him.

"I am glad you found the dojo. We will be training in here tomorrow morning. I would like to see you here at half-past seven in the morning for Tai Chi before breakfast!" With that, he made a small formal bow, which they returned respectfully. Then he smiled at them, turned and left.

"Seven-thirty?" groaned Charlie. "I thought they might let us have a bit of a holiday whilst we are here."

Mark shook his head, gravely. "This isn't a holiday, Charlie. I rather think it is more serious than anything we have done so far."

Charlie recovered from his disappointment quickly. "All the more reason to get to know our new environment!" he grinned. "Let the tour continue!"

James and Malcolm were even more proud to show off the grounds of the castle and the countryside that surrounded it. They took their friends down to the shores of the Loch where they played at skimming stones on its smooth surface. Then they went for a long walk around the edge of the Loch and then headed up into the mountains beyond. The boys enjoyed introducing their friends to their favourite tracks and places. It was a beautiful December afternoon, and the weather was kind to them.

"Don't ever get caught up here in the snow," warned James. "It can come in from the mountains very quickly, and before you know it, you are lost in a sea of freezing white."

"Oh yes!" cried Malcolm. "It's very dangerous to be out here in the mist too. You can lose your way very easily and get stuck up here. When the mist comes in off the Loch, you can't see your hand in front of your face!"

The students made a mental note to avoid these dangerous conditions. It sounded rather scary.

"Does the monster ever come out of the Loch?" asked Nell.

James and Malcolm laughed. "Well, we don't know for sure that there actually is a monster. But if there is one, I expect it stays in the Loch," said James.

"Except when it gets hungry, and there is a tasty looking snack on the shore," said Malcolm, wickedly teasing Nell, who had clearly got it in her head that the Loch had a monster and was resolved to torture herself with terror stories.

Nell squeaked. This Loch monster was scary!

Mark laughed. "There isn't a monster, Nell. They are just teasing you. The only monsters we have to worry about are the Shadowlands ninjas – and we seem to keep getting the better of them. So there isn't much to worry about!"

Chapter 23

After a pleasant night in their new rooms in the Turret, the students all gathered for Tai Chi in the Ballroom. They were all a bit sleepy, having stayed up talking and laughing, excited to be sleeping in these remarkable circular rooms in this amazing old castle.

"Just as well we are going to wake you up with some Tai Chi!" said Sensei Goodwin with a smile. "You lot don't look good for much yet this morning. Let's take you into the day gently."

The students spread out and followed Sensei Goodwin as he led them through the Tai Chi sequence. Multiple reflections of themselves shone back from the mirrors that encased the Ballroom. They found it interesting to watch themselves moving through the Tai Chi. For the first time, they began to realise that they were learning to move like martial artists. There was something rather beautiful about it.

Tai Chi only lasted twenty minutes or so, and they tucked into a hearty breakfast afterwards. Lady Norma was a great believer in a good breakfast, and she clucked around them, helping them to porridge, plates of fried vegetable patties, potato hashes and baked beans. Then there were freshly made bread buns with bowls of preserved fruits.

"That should set you up for the day!" proclaimed Lady Norma. "A great warrior marches on his breakfast."

"Doesn't that make rather a mess?" asked Charlie cheekily.

Lady Norma chuckled and ruffled his hair. "Well if he makes a mess, he will have to clean it up – no matter how big and important a warrior he is!"

When breakfast was over, and all had eaten their fill, James and Malcolm took their friends round to the stables where they were met by Lord Wallace, Sergeant Yeald and Sensei Tanaka. He was there already when they arrived, checking on the tack of over a dozen horses that were standing outside their stables, picking at hay nets.

"I thought we would start your stay here with an orientation ride into the mountains. You have to get to know your environment. You might be forced to flee to the mountains at any time, so you should know where you are going – and how to get back!" he added with a chuckle. "There is no better way to see the countryside than on horseback, and I have some fine friends here who will be

154

happy to take you."

Carlotta looked horrified. She really didn't want to get on a horse. Lord Wallace had been warned that she was very afraid of horses, but he knew about what had happened to her mother and understood that it was the idea of falling off one that bothered her, not the horse itself.

Sergeant Yeald spoke gently, but firmly. "Carlotta, I know this is a big thing for you, but I really must insist that you try. Everyone is here for your safety, but there is still a chance you will have to ride away from the castle at some point. You need to know where you are going."

Lord Wallace led forward a large cob mare. She was patched in brown, black and white and had a massive fluffy mane and tail. "This is Duchess. She is our safest, more sensible horse. She loves young people and will look after you. We call her our Nanny horse because she looks after her riders so well. Will you come and meet her?"

Carlotta swallowed hard. All eyes were on her. Every nerve in her body was on edge as she stepped forward. She didn't want to do this, but she knew that she must. Everyone was risking their lives to look after her. She owed it to them. That didn't stop her feeling terrified, though. Duchess appeared oblivious to all this. The horse looked beyond it to the sweet girl beneath the trembling surface. She dropped her big lovely head, pressed it gently to Carlotta's chest and breathed deeply. Carlotta reached forward a tentative hand and stroked the side of her head. Duchess gave a low, gentle whicker. The rumbling of it and the scent of the warm horse stirred something in Carlotta's memory – a happier memory from before the accident that had taken her mother. Carlotta felt a deep sadness well up in her. She didn't want to cry in front of everyone, so she bent her head forward and hid her face in Duchess' great forelock. She found comfort in that moment.

"Let's get you aboard, shall we?" said Lord Wallace with a look of compassion. He was a man with a highly developed sense of empathy. He knew how horses felt just by being with them, and he knew what humans felt too. He ran down the stirrups and turned to Carlotta. She backed away. Lord Wallace wasn't surprised by this. He thought maybe it would be too much for her, but he wanted to give her the opportunity.

"I'm sorry. I just can't," said Carlotta quietly. She wanted to try; she wanted to trust this lovely big horse. But as soon as she thought about getting on the horse, her heart started racing again, and her mind was full of torturous images of accidents and falling off. She stood there, shaking and struggling to maintain control. The urge to cry and run away was strong. But she didn't give in to it.

"How about you stay and do some martial arts training with me this afternoon?" Sensei Goodwin had appeared from nowhere and was now smiling at Carlotta. She nodded gratefully. "Yes please, Sensei. I think I would prefer that."

Lord Wallace then looked at the other students, deciding which horse to pair each with. He selected black fell ponies for David and Charlie and a bay mare called Waverley for Mark. Gina and Nell were put up on Highland Ponies, and Lucy was given a dark bay mare called Josie.

"That just leaves Rupert for you, Xinia!" said Lord Wallace. "I hear you are a very accomplished horsewoman. Rupert here is a lovely fellow, very sensitive but sensible too. Sensei Tanaka here tells me you are the best of the riders, so I think you will appreciate him."

He led forward a gleaming bay thoroughbred with a narrow white stripe down his face. "He used to be a racehorse," said Lord Wallace. "When his career was over, we took him in here. I think he likes running in the Scottish hills a whole lot more than he liked running round in circles on racetracks!"

Xinia stepped forward and said hello to Rupert. She offered her hand for him to sniff. He gave it an experimental lick and mouthed it with his lips. She smiled and then moved her hands up his face, rubbing slowly and talking to him in a low voice. She stroked along his neck and gradually moved in to wrap her arms around his neck and press her face into his short black mane as she hugged him. She felt him relax as she rubbed his shoulders. Then she stood at his side and placed her hands on front of and behind the saddle, looking for an indication of comfort and consent from him. After thinking about it a second, Rupert dropped the remaining tension in his back and moved slightly sideways towards Xinia. She smiled; she could feel what he was saying to her in that moment, what he was giving to her. "Good boy," she said. "Thank you." Then she stepped lightly up into the saddle and settled very gently on his back. She leant forward, whispering to him and rubbing the base of his neck. His ears flickered back, listening to her.

Lord Wallace noted the skill and understanding with which Xinia had introduced herself to Rupert. He remembered Xinia's mother and what a remarkable horsewoman she had been. He could see that her daughter had inherited her gift.

He turned to Sergeant Yeald. "We have Samson here for you. He is a fine fellow – an excellent horse. Used to be a drum horse." He led forward a sizeable heavy horse for Sergeant Yeald.

"Perfect, dear boy! Fine fellow indeed!" observed Sergeant Yeald. "I think we are going to be firm friends!" He gave Samson's neck a rub and scratched the base of his mane when he tilted his neck to one side to request it. Once the scratching started, Samson stretched his head out, turned his neck even more and pulled a face of exquisite pleasure as Sergeant Yeald scratched the itchy bit. The students all laughed. They hadn't seen a horse do that before.

Last of all, Lord Wallace brought forward a black warmblood horse for Sensei Tanaka. The horse was of medium weight, with strong, sleek muscles and a shining black coat. "This is Ashby," Lord Wallace introduced the fine horse to Sensei Tanaka. "I think you will enjoy him very much. He is one of my special favourites." Lord

Wallace chuckled. "They all are, in fact!"

Having matched everyone with a suitable horse friend, he led them out into a large paddock.

"Before we set off into the hills, I want to see you all ride for a bit to check I have you all matched up appropriately. So let's warm up with a few circuits and circles, then I want to see each of you canter along the bottom edge of the field."

They did as they were bid. Lord Wallace assessed the seats and experience of each of the students. They all did well enough trotting around, and he could see that some sat more naturally and with more skill than others. Sergeant Yeald and Sensei Tanaka joined in the exercise, and the students were impressed to see what excellent horsemen they were. "I will ride like that one day," thought Mark.

Then it was time for them to canter the length of the field. Charlie and David set off first on their matching black fell ponies. They made it across the field okay, although it was clear they were fairly new to riding. Then Mark set off after them on Waverley. This was not so successful, though. He made it halfway across the field, but then Waverley dropped a shoulder, sending Mark tumbling over the top and off to the side. Mark was surprised to find that he flew straight into the kind of front roll that he had been taught in the dojo during Aikido lessons. He realised at that moment the connection between martial arts and horse-riding. He was thankful to find that he rolled easily and back onto his feet with no harm done.

Lord Wallace chuckled. "She is up to her old tricks again!" He caught Waverley up and asked Lucy to try her instead. Lucy hopped off her horse and onto Waverley and tried to canter her across the meadow. The same thing happened. Halfway across, Waverley slipped in a cheeky shoulder drop and away came Lucy, tumbling to the soft meadow just as Mark had. She was similarly relieved to find that she was projected into a front roll that circled her back to her feet in a moment. This was ninja horse-riding at it's best!

Xinia watched all this, noting the shoulder drop. She liked the look of this horse who obviously had her own ideas about who she was going to let ride her. She turned to Lord Wallace. "Can I try please, Sir?" she asked.

"If you can ride her to the top of the field and back, you can have her for the ride today," he said.

161

Xinia hopped off Rupert and passed his reins to Mark, who was the only one without a horse now. Xinia hopped up on Waverley and urged her quickly into a fast canter up the hill. Waverley sensed she now had a rider who not only knew what she was doing, but was fearless also. Nevertheless, she decided to test her anyway with her shoulder drop trick. Xinia saw the thought cross Waverley's mind. She saw it as a picture projected on the inside of her own mind. So she was ready for it when it came. She sat back, adjusting her weight and leaving the horse's front quarters free to do as they wished. The shoulder drop came and went a couple of times before Waverley decided that this trick wouldn't work. Waverley began to see Xinia's mind as Xinia saw hers. As they raced together up the meadow, horse and girl became one – one in body and one in mind. When they cantered steadily back, both horse and girl had a slightly glassy look in their eyes. Lord Wallace recognised this. He knew what had happened between them.

"I think Waverley has chosen her rider," he said with a smile.

Meanwhile, Mark had been left holding Rupert. Having heard about his history as a racehorse, Mark felt somewhat inadequate to the task of being this horse's partner. He hadn't been riding long, and this horse was a lot more experienced than he was. He stood with his back to Rupert, watching Xinia, not quite sure how to go about introducing himself to him. Rupert actually quite liked this approach. After a while, he took a step forward and nudged his nose into the back of Mark's elbow. Mark felt this but didn't dare ruin the moment by turning around. They stood like this a while, and gradually Rupert stepped forward until his head was over Mark's arm. Mark cupped his arm under Rupert's jaw and gently tickled his cheek with his other hand. Then slowly he turned and faced him, taking care not to stare him straight in the eyes, as Sensei Tanaka had taught them. He rubbed along Rupert's neck as he had seen Xinia do, then copied her subtle way of asking for consent. He placed his hands either side of Rupert's saddle and rubbed gently at the fur there. Rupert thought about it again for a moment before relaxing his back and pressing sideways into Mark. Mark accepted this invitation and very carefully climbed up into the saddle, making sure to lower himself into it quietly.

Lord Wallace watched this with surprise. He had thought it likely that Xinia would be capable of gaining this horse's trust because he knew how good her mother had been and the special talents that ran in her family. He hadn't expected this young lad to be so sensitive to the horse.

"Well, it looks like Rupert has accepted you, Mark. Well done. Let's all head off into the mountains now and see where the day and the trails take us!"

Chapter 24

Carlotta and Sensei Goodwin watched the others ride out down the track and disappear out of sight. Carlotta was relieved that she hadn't been made to go with them. Sensei Goodwin stood at her side, holding Duchess' reins.

"Let's go and take Duchess to the paddock, shall we?" suggested Sensei Goodwin.

Carlotta nodded and followed as he led Duchess into the small paddock near the stable block. He removed the saddle and bridle and hung them on the fence. Then he gave her a friendly stroke on the shoulders before whispering to her, "Don't go too far, my friend!"

Carlotta heard this. She had been relieved to see the tack removed, but that last comment suggested her time with the horse may not be over for the day.

"Are we going to go to the ballroom to do martial arts?" asked Carlotta, keen to get herself away from the stables and free of further interaction with horses.

Sensei Goodwin smiled. He knew exactly what she was angling for. "Well it is such a fine day, I thought we might do some training outdoors – here in fact!"

Carlotta looked suspicious. But whilst this was about martial arts rather than horses, she couldn't object.

"Let's start with some breathing exercises," said Sensei Goodwin. "Right now, your pulse is probably racing because you are worrying about the horse riding. Am I right?"

She nodded. How did Sensei Goodwin always seem to know what she was thinking and feeling?!

"As you will have realised by now, there are different types of martial arts. They differ in all sorts of ways, in fact. Some are designed to work well when your pulse is racing, and your blood is laced with adrenaline. These arts have big and simple movements. Other arts involve smaller and more complicated movements. They require your brain to be cool, your pulse to be lower and your adrenaline low or at least under control. Aikido is one such art. It involves doing clever things – clever things with your mind, intricate movements with your hands and feet which co-ordinate and facilitate it all. So to be good at Aikido and harness it's power, you need to learn to control yourself, to control your pulse and adrenaline. The best way to do this

166

is by learning to control your breath."

"Control my breath, Sensei?" This sounded like a strange idea to Carlotta. "I breathe all the time!"

"This will be easier to learn by doing it," assured Sensei Goodwin. "Let's give it a try. Right now, your pulse is higher due to the fear you felt a little earlier. So let's use that as an opportunity to learn. Copy me."

Carlotta stood opposite Sensei Goodwin, taking up the same stance as him, her feet shoulder-width apart and her knees slightly bent, as she had been taught to do in previous classes.

"Place your hands on the middle of your abdomen so you can feel it when you breathe in and out. Then we are going to take five deep breaths, breathing in deeply through the nose, holding the breath just a second and then breathing all the way out through the mouth. Try it!" said Sensei Goodwin.

Carlotta copied him. Her hands on her middle, she could feel as the breath filled her lungs as she breathed in. She felt a bit silly just standing there taking deep breaths, but by the fifth one, she did notice that she felt a bit calmer.

Perhaps there was something in this?

"Now, let's add some arms," said Sensei Goodwin. "Arms in front and lowered to start with. Then as you breathe in, raise your arms up and then spread them wide at your sides. It will help open up your lungs, and you will feel the breath in a different way."

Carlotta tried this. At first, she just tried to get the arm movement right and synchronise it with her breathing. But after a while, she began to feel that the air she breathed in seemed to energise the whole of her upper body, spreading along her arms to her hands. Her hands felt a bit warm and tingly. Carlotta smiled, liking this feeling. She was so absorbed in it that she had now forgotten about feeling anxious.

"And relax," Sensei Goodwin drew the exercise to a stop. "Feeling better now?"

Carlotta smiled. "Yes, Sensei! Much!"

"Then let's do something more fun. Do you remember how to roll?"

"I think so Sensei," said Carlotta, a little unsure because

168

there had been so much to learn since she had joined the Academy.

"Let's have a little refresher, shall we? Run at me and try to chop me on the head. I will then gently project you, and you will do a forward roll and land back on your feet. I seem to remember you did this well last time we did it in class."

"Oh yes – I remember now Sensei," said Carlotta. Sensei Goodwin nodded to her, and she ran at him, her arm raised to chop him on the head. He pivoted out of her line of attack, but took her raised arm and gently guided her to ground with it. Before she knew it, she had rolled across the grass and back up onto her feet. She turned and gave a big smile, pleased with herself. Sensei Goodwin nodded. He was pleased she had remembered so well.

"Again!" he said. Once again, Carlotta ran at him and was sent rolling away. They repeated this almost a dozen times before he stopped.

"I think we can safely say that you can do that. Now let's make this more interesting."

Sensei Goodwin fetched a wooden box from nearby. "Now

try that again, but this time run to the box, step up onto it and I will project you from there."

He stood behind the box so that she was running straight at him. With her last step, she stepped up onto the box. At that point, he pivoted again and used her arm to guide her to the ground. She made the roll completely safely and was soon up and turning to repeat the exercise.

After a few repeats, Sensei Goodwin got her to stand on the box on her own and then project herself forward into a roll. "This is harder," said Carlotta. "It's one thing for someone else to throw you, but it's hard to throw yourself!"

"Don't think about the ground, think about the roll," said Sensei Goodwin. "This is where your breath can help. Take a deep breath, fill your body with energy. Then see that energy flowing forward off the box and circling through the roll. Breathe out as you go with that energy."

Carlotta breathed deeply and imagined her body filling with light and then a stream of fireworks circling out of her chest and through a roll. Having visualised it, she then breathed out and tumbled forward off the box, her arm curved to meet the ground and project her through the roll. The extra height at the start of the roll sent her tumbling

170

faster and with more momentum. She found it easier to regain her standing position at the end of the roll.

"Well done! Really good!" Sensei Goodwin was pleased and encouraging her. "You curved your arm really nicely, and it took you into a very elegant roll." He paused. "Now, do you think you could manage a dozen more of those?"

"A dozen?" queried Carlotta. "Oh boy!"

Sensei Goodwin laughed. "Repetition is the mother of success! We have to train your auto-pilot. But you can take your time. I would rather you took lots of breaks than have you rush this. It's important to practise things well. Never practise things badly!"

So Carlotta did as she was bid. Each time, she paused on the box, taking deep breaths, visualising and being sure to curve her arm just as she had that first time to ensure a smooth connection to the ground as she made contact with it.

Eventually, Sensei Goodwin decided she had had enough. Carlotta didn't know if she had done the exercise another dozen times or not. She had become so focussed on what she was doing; she had lost count.

"Very good! Very good! You really know how to approach the ground and not be hurt by it now, don't you?"

"I think so Sensei..." Carlotta wasn't a boastful girl, but she knew she had done a good job of the exercise.

"Take a little break and do some more deep breathing. I am going to fetch a friend to help us with the next exercise."

Sensei Goodwin left her to her breathing and went into the field to fetch Duchess, who had been watching the afternoon's class with mild interest. He put her bridle on and led her back out to where Carlotta was doing her breathing.

"Am I right in thinking that your fear of horses was about falling off them?" asked Sensei Goodwin directly. He was a man who saw through the complexities of many things and got straight to the point. Carlotta was used to people being afraid to speak directly to her about her fear, so she was surprised at his directness.

"Yes, Sensei," she said, answering a straight question with a straight answer.

"Well, we know that you can fall without hurting yourself

172

now, don't we?"

His logic was hard to argue with.

"Well, yes..." Carlotta trailed off.

"And you saw how the other students just did the same sort of rolls that you have been practising all afternoon when they fell off Waverley?"

"Yes, Sensei," agreed Carlotta.

"So what is there to worry about?" asked Sensei Goodwin.

Carlotta thought about this a moment. "Well, it's higher up from a horse. It's further to fall. And I don't want the horse to fall on me, like it did on my mother."

"Ah, well if you roll away from it, the horse isn't likely to fall on you. All things are possible of course with horses, but there is a lot we can do to keep the risk to the minimum. The most important thing is that we know you can fall safely and roll away. So let's give that a try. I'm not going to ask you to ride Duchess. I just want you to sit on her a moment. Then, when you are ready, I want you to tumble forward over her shoulder. She's a good girl. She will stand quietly for you."

"You don't mind helping us out, do you, Duchess?" Sensei Goodwin asked the big horse. He gave her neck a rub, and she leaned into it.

Carlotta looked very doubtful about all this. But again, she couldn't fault Sensei Goodwin's logic. She looked at the big horse. Could she do this? Dare she?

Carlotta decided that she could. Taking a deep breath to steady her nerves, she nodded to Sensei Goodwin, placed her hands on Duchess' back and raised her left leg off the ground for Sensei Goodwin to give her a leg up onto Duchess' back.

Once she was there, she held onto the base of Duchess' mane. She had ridden a lot before her mother's accident, so it was not unfamiliar for her to be on a horse. But her pulse was racing now she was there. Her mind started filling up with bad memories and thoughts.

"Stop that," said Sensei Goodwin, who knew what she was feeling and thinking. It was all to be expected, but he knew he had to redirect her. "Close your eyes and take deep breaths, in through your nose and out through your mouth. Empty your mind. Just concentrate on the breath, feel it energise you, feel it fill you with power. Now let go of her mane and raise your arms and then move them out to the side as you breathe. You are sitting perfectly well. There is no need to hang on to her."

Carlotta had learned to trust Sensei Goodwin. He had taught her many things now, and she had never got hurt. She found the feeling of trust comforting. She hung onto that peaceful feeling as she did the breathing exercises. As she drew the air into her lungs, she visualised her body filling with light. She became so relaxed, she had almost entirely forgotten that she was sitting on a horse.

"Open your eyes," said Sensei Goodwin. "Then I want you to lean forward over her left shoulder, extend your arm but keep that curve in it. And let yourself tumble forward to the ground and into a roll. See what you are going to do and then do it. The mind leads the body!"

Carlotta didn't give herself too much time to think about it. She knew that the more she thought about this, the harder and more impossible it would become. So she took a deep breath, lent forward and reached for the ground. Her mind flew ahead of her body, imagining the light from her chest flowing out of her arm, circling down and across the grass. A second later, her body had followed her mind, and she was back on her feet having tumbled from the back of

Duchess, through a forward roll and back up again. Carlotta stood there, looking stunned. She couldn't believe what she had done!

Sensei Goodwin gave her a beaming smile. He knew it had taken a lot for her to do that.

"Well done! Absolutely fantastic! I knew you could do it!"

Carlotta's face lit up. She was proud of herself. It hadn't been easy, but she had done it.

"Now you know what I am going to say now, don't you?" Sensei Goodwin said, still smiling.

"Again?" asked Carlotta.

"Again! And again! And again!" was the reply.

Duchess stood as still as a rock whilst Carlotta repeatedly climbed onto her back and then tumbled through forward rolls to the ground. When Sensei Goodwin finally called a halt to the lesson, Carlotta put her arms around Duchess' neck and kissed it. "Thank you, Duchess," she said.

"I think Duchess has earned a rest in her field, don't you? Why don't you take her back there?" Sensei Goodwin handed Duchess' reins to Carlotta before she could question the idea.

Carlotta only hesitated a moment, just long enough for her brain to catch up with her afternoon's activities. When it did, she realised that she had nothing left to be fearful about when it came to horses. Something dark had lifted from Carlotta, and now she realised it. She felt very grateful to this gentle, great horse for helping her release her fears. Reaching her hand out, she gently stroked Duchess' face, feeling the fur like velvet beneath her fingers. She traced her fingers lightly up between Duchess' eyes and across her forehead. Duchess liked this and dropped her head to ask for more of it. Carlotta found herself enjoying stroking a horse again. It had been so long since she had done this. But the magic was still there.

She smiled as she stroked Duchess. "Thank you, girl. Let's take you back to your field, shall we?"

Carlotta turned to thank Sensei Goodwin, but he had disappeared. She didn't see him in the woods nearby, but he had watched with great satisfaction whilst she had stroked the horse. He knew his work was done.

Chapter 25

Lord Wallace led the ride out along the tracks and up into the mountains. This was the first time most of the students had ridden out in the countryside, and they were a bit nervous about it at first. But they were also excited.

It soon became clear that the horses knew the mountains and were relaxed in this rich environment with so much to see and experience. Even Rupert, the former racehorse that Mark was riding, was sure-footed on the terrain and was very calm and happy.

After they had climbed a little way into the mountains, Lord Wallace drew the riders to a stop on a grassy platform to the side of the track that afforded a fine view over the Loch. He beamed with pride in the beauty of the land that was his home. "From here, we can see the mountain pass climbing up to our left and the Loch stretching several miles to the West. And if you look back to the right, you will see we also have a good view of the castle and the approaching road. We call this Heather Ridge, because it is edged in the most beautiful bright purple heather that you can see from the castle itself."

The students gazed at the views, marvelling in the

magnificence. This was big country: big mountains, big Loch, big views that stretched for miles and miles. They had never seen anything like it before.

"My Mum would like to see this," commented Mark.

A lot of the other students agreed that their parents, family and friends would love this place. Mark noticed that Charlie was strangely silent, which was unlike him. He wondered why. Charlie usually had so much to say.

"Onwards and upwards!" called Lord Wallace. "I want to take you up to the Blue Caves, and our time is short. It will get dark at about four o'clock. That is the first lesson you need to learn about this area. It gets dark earlier than in the south. You don't want to get caught up in the mountains in the dark. So always aim to get back to the castle a couple of hours before dark, just in case something slows you down. This is wild country. Many things can happen..." he trailed off slightly ominously. The students heard the warning in his words, though.

He led the ride back onto the track, which wound and climbed around and up the mountain. Again and again, Mark and his friends were amazed by the new and beautiful views down across the Loch and to the mountains beyond. Their horses picked their way along the path, carrying them easily and moving together as a herd.

Shortly after midday, they reached the highest point of their climb. Lord Wallace drew his horse to a stop outside the entrance to a large cave. "This is the entrance to the Blue Caves. It leads to a network of caves that go deep into the mountain. I don't advise you to go very far into them, but the entrance cave will shelter you from the weather if you should ever find yourself out here in need of it."

"Why are they called the Blue Caves?" asked Charlie, who Mark noticed was back to his normal self now.

"It's because they contain a special mineral that is blue. They aren't mined these days, but in the past they were. There are seams of sparkling blue crystal in there. If you are lucky, you will see them glinting in the cavern walls."

"Can we go in, please, Sir?" asked Lucy, who wanted to see the blue crystals.

Lord Wallace looked up at the sky and pulled a face that indicated some degree of reluctance. "The sun is over the yardarm, so we only have a few hours before darkness falls. We must make our way back very soon. But it wouldn't harm to let you take a few minutes to look around. Don't be long, though!"

He dismounted and reached into his pocket before producing a small torch. He offered it to Lucy, who slid from her horse in a flash and gladly accepted it.

"What about the horses?" said Lucy, realising that she couldn't just abandon her horse to go and look in a cave.

"I suggest that half of you go and take a look in the cave whilst the other half holds their own horse and someone else's. Then you can swap. That way, everyone will be able to take a look inside, and the horses will all be kept safe. We don't want them wandering off and having accidents!"

"Don't be long now! Five minutes per party, please!" Lord Wallace warned them.

Mark, Charlie, David, Lucy and Xinia went in first. Scrabbling around the loose rocks at the entrance to the cave, they followed the surprisingly powerful beam of the torch into the pitch black. The cavern was large. At the back, they could see an opening to a tunnel.

Lucy shone the torch on the walls towards the back of the

cave. "Wow!" she exclaimed.

"Oh my goodness! It's so pretty!" said Xinia. The walls sparkled with blue crystals. As the torchlight caught them, they sparkled and shone.

The boys were impressed too. "I have never seen anything like this!" proclaimed David.

"Just wow!" agreed Charlie.

"This would be a brilliant place to camp out in an emergency," commented Mark, who was less impressed by the crystals than he was the potential of the cave itself. "This could come in really handy one day. Let's ask if we can bring some equipment up here for emergencies."

Sergeant Yeald had wandered in behind them to make his own checks of the location. "Good thinking, Mark! Whilst Carlotta is here, anything could happen. We should equip this place as a safe room – somewhere to run to if we have to get her away from the castle. I will speak with Wallace about it. I am sure he will agree it is a fine plan!"

"A fine plan indeed!" he repeated thoughtfully to himself as he walked out of the cave.

After the second group had gone into the cave to take a look, it was time to head back. Lord Wallace was clearly very keen to get going, so they didn't hold him up long.

"That looked fun!" Charlie called back to Mark.

"It looked jolly useful too!" agreed Mark. "Let's hope we never need it. We should definitely equip it as a hideout."

"I would like to go back and see the blue crystals again," Lucy called from behind. "They were gorgeous!"

"Wow yes," agreed Xinia. "I hope we come back here soon."

"I'm sure we will," assured Mark. "Lord Wallace said we would come back."

Lord Wallace heard all the chatter going on amongst the riders behind him. He smiled. He was glad they were enjoying themselves and were so keen to explore his beloved mountains.

Sensei Tanaka and Sergeant Yeald kept up their position at the back of the ride. They rode quietly, not saying much. They were pleased that the students were enjoying the ride, but they were here for serious reasons. For Sensei Tanaka and Sergeant Yeald, this was a reconnaissance exercise. They were here to map out the countryside in preparation for whatever events might yet transpire.

Sergeant Yeald was keen to get back to the castle. He had left Carlotta in the care of Sensei Goodwin and knew she would be safe. But it had been hard for him to leave his Principal and he knew he would feel better when she was back in his sight.

Chapter 26

Life at Shadowlands had become even more grim since the failed kidnap attempt. Instructor Jack Adams was in a perpetually foul mood. The slightest thing sent him into furious rants, and he dished out cruel punishments for almost random reasons. All the students trod extremely carefully, trying to avoid igniting his anger or giving him a reason to notice them. It was always safer not to be noticed. They soon learned that getting noticed typically led to getting punished.

They had hardly seen the headmaster since the night of the failed abduction. He occasionally floated past in the distance, but he paid no attention to them. They were beneath his notice since failing to perform their mission. The students were miserable.

Today, Instructor Adams had his students lined up and standing to attention on the concrete parade ground. He paced up and down in front of them, as was his habit. Fury such as his was unable to stand still. It drove his pacing, but never seemed to relent.

"So you are telling me that a dozen of you were unable to get past one little old man?" he quizzed them in disbelief.

The students hung their heads, reluctant to attract his attention by answering his question.

"Answer me when I ask you a question!" Instructor Adams roared at them. "Did a dozen of you fail to get past one little old man?"

This time the students didn't dare stay silent. "Yes, Sir!"

"How? Why? What did he do?"

The students looked down again. Instructor Adams intended to get to the bottom of this matter. He needed to know where the training had failed. He had taught them to fight and to attack. Twelve of them should have easily been capable of taking on one man. He poked one of the boys in the chest. "You, tell me now. What happened?"

"He just kept moving around, Sir."

Instructor Adams stopped and stared at the boy, incredulously. "He kept moving around?! What sort of explanation is that?! Why didn't you hit him?"

"We tried to, Sir!" protested the boy. "He just wasn't there. And we kept falling over."

186

"You kept falling over?!" Instructor Adams was so angry and disgusted at this account; he kept repeating what he was being told with outraged disbelief.

He poked another student. "Is this true?"

"Yes, Sir," said the next boy. "He kept moving, and we all just kept missing him and banging into each other and falling over."

"How?!" roared Instructor Adams. "You aren't falling over now. I have never seen you falling over. But twelve of you fell over at the same time? I don't believe it!" He resumed his pacing. "Of all the stupid, clumsy, idiotic..."

He was so angry now that he couldn't finish his sentence. His face white with rage, he was trying to decide now between punishing them and teaching them. He decided on both. He walked to the end of the line and around the back of the students. Then, with no warning, he walked along the back of the line, giving each student a sharp shove. One by one, they fell forward. He moved so quickly that they were all on the ground before they could think to evade his shove. There were a few cries as they hit the hard concrete, and there were a lot of grazed knees.

"Silence!" he snapped. "Now get up! We are going to learn how to stay on our feet and not be so easily toppled."

He proceeded to teach them how to stand and move to achieve maximum stability. They were so relieved to have passed beyond the yelling and the punishments parts of today's activities that they worked hard on this training. Nevertheless, after an hour or more of standing and shuffling, they were desperate for a break. Finally, Instructor Adams called a stop to it.

"You, come here," he called one of the students out. "Try and push me over."

He took up the stance he had taught them, his feet shoulder-width apart, one ahead of the other pointing forward and the other pointing to the two o'clock position. He bent his knees and settled his weight low between his feet. The student, a large, strong boy, tried to push him over from the front. He placed his hands on Instructor Adams shoulders and pushed with all his strength. He was unable to move him, though.

"Now try from the sides and from behind," ordered the instructor.

The boy tried again, pushing the instructor from the side and from behind. Each time, he was unable to move him an inch.

"See? If you have the right stance, you are stable and can't be easily moved or pushed over. Get into pairs and practise this. I don't want to see anyone getting pushed over!"

Chapter 27

The Academy students were having a much nicer time than the Shadowlands students. Their days were filled with horse riding, martial arts lessons in the ballroom of the castle, Ninja Skills lessons in the mountains and bodyguarding lessons and drills with Sergeant Yeald. To the students' delight, the teachers of the ordinary academic subjects had not made the journey up to Scotland, so there were no regular school lessons.

True to his word, Sergeant Yeald taught them how to escort a Principal away from an attack and how to exit a building. After breakfast one morning, he took them on a tour around the rooms of the castle, pointing out routes and exits and teaching them as he went.

"An attack can be indoors or outdoors. When it happens, the chief bodyguard doesn't take on the attackers. As we practised back at the Academy, the chief bodyguard's job is to get the principal away to safety, leaving the team to take on the attackers. Now, the question is, where does the chief bodyguard take his principal? That will depend on where he is. Hopefully, he would have a radio and a car waiting, and he can get on the radio and say that he needs urgent assistance and then seek to get his principal into the car.

Out here in the Scottish Highlands, this may not be possible.

"A bodyguard should always be completely aware of his surroundings. That means more than just being aware of what is in the room he currently occupies. He must be aware of where every door leads, all the possible exits from that room and the building and all possible dangers. He must also know what lies beyond all these exits. He must know what is outside the building, what is in the area around the building and have some places in mind that he could take his principal to in the event of an attack. Fortune favours the prepared mind. Always have a plan. Always have several plans.

"Now, if you are coming out of a sterile area – one that has been checked for problems – directly you come out of that door, there can be snipers or lurking attackers. You have to assume that there is danger everywhere. So you want to get that person into a vehicle.

"Say you are going from a hotel to a car, your principal is in danger between the hotel and the car. When the car is moving, you are relatively safe. But directly that car stops, you are in danger again. So you want to keep moving.

"Use your time here well. Normally a good house guest wouldn't go exploring the castle uninvited. But you have been invited here as bodyguards. That means it is part of your job to explore everywhere. Make sure that you know every room, corridor and exit from the castle. When you are out in the countryside, use that opportunity to learn the layout of the land. Learn the routes and learn the places you might take cover or hide."

Charlie put his hand up. "Like the Blue Caves, Sir?"

"Absolutely, dear boy. They are a significant land feature for you on this mission. You could use them as a place to escape to, a place to hide, a place to meet up."

Mark raised his hand next. "I think we should take some equipment and supplies up there, Sir, so we have everything we need if we have to hide out there."

"Excellent plan. Good fellow. Let's speak to Lord and Lady Wallace and see what can be rustled up. Then we can ride up to the caves and take the supplies there."

Over lunch, Sergeant Yeald spoke with their hosts and outlined the students plan to equip the Blue Caves as a hideout. Lord and Lady Wallace agreed this was an excellent idea, and the afternoon was spent assembling everything that might be needed. The students helped, fetching and carrying things and packing everything away in bags that could be tied to their backs and saddles. They had brought everything to the Ballroom and were laying out everything in squares on the floor.

Sensei Tanaka moved amongst them, nodding approvingly as they laid kit out before packing it away. He had taught them this skill in their Assessment Course and was delighted to see they had remembered it. He showed them how to roll bedding in tight rolls, tied with string to keep them as compact as possible.

"Now, what sort of food do you think you will need up there?" asked Lady Wallace.

"I think cans of beans would be best," said Mark decidedly. He had given this a lot of thought already.

"And cans of soup," interjected Lucy. "Soup is tasty, and if you heat it on a stove, it is very warming."

"So we will need a can opener and stove," pointed out Xinia.

"Ah, no problem. We have lots of camping equipment here. You have a choice of stoves, in fact," offered Lord Wallace.

"I think it is best we take the smallest one as we have to carry it up to the caves," decided Mark.

"We will need bowls and spoons too!" pointed out Charlie. "And I think we need some crackers to go with the soup."

"Won't they get eaten by the wildlife if we leave them in the cave?" asked Xinia.

Lady Wallace smiled. "Not if you put them in a good tin! It just so happens I have one. And I bet we could find another tin to fill with Shortbread!"

The students all agreed that a tin of Shortbread would be a fine addition to their plans.

By dinner time, everything that they needed for their expedition the next day had been located and packed. They were ready for their next adventure!

Chapter 28

Breakfast was a very early affair on the day of the trek up to the Blue Caves. The students had risen just before sunrise, eaten their breakfast and were down to the stables as the sun was streaming over the mountains.

Mark was there first. He found Lord Wallace carrying a bale of hay into the small paddock near the stables. In the paddock were a small, black, shaggy, Shetland pony and a larger horse who had dramatic black and white markings.

"Who are they, Sir?" asked Mark, who hadn't seen these horses before. The black and white horse eyed him suspiciously and took a step back.

"This is Stumpy the Shetland Pony. He is here to keep the other horse company. His name is Zeebee."

"Is he coming on the ride today?" asked Mark. He liked the look of this horse. There was a kind of light around him. Mark couldn't quite put his finger on it, but he had the strangest of thoughts when he looked at him. The thought was *That's my horse!* Mark knew this was a ridiculous thing to think because he had only just met him, and very clearly, this was one of Lord Wallace's horses. Still, Mark could imagine having a horse like this as his own.

"Definitely not!" laughed Lord Wallace. "He is a long way off being ready for that. He is here in the paddock today to help him get a bit more used to people. He has had a hard time in life and is of the firm opinion that humans are horrible and likely to hurt him. So we have to gently persuade him that not all humans are horrible and that he is safe now. He can't learn that out on the back pasture where he doesn't see anyone. So I have brought him in. Perhaps you would like to help me teach him that people can be nice?"

"Oh my goodness! I would love to!" gasped Mark. "That would be amazing! I have never helped train a horse before!"

"Well, this bit is very simple but very important," explained Lord Wallace. "I want you to come and see him as often as possible and just spend time with him doing nothing. Just stand at the fence. Ignore him at first. You can turn your back to him, in fact. Don't give him your focus because that will make him feel worried. But just be there. Don't try and feed him at first. We will get to that once he is ready to touch you. Do you think you could do that?"

"Yes, Sir! I most definitely can!" Mark was very keen to get started. "Shall I start now?"

"No, come later when things are quiet, and you can spend some time relaxing with him. Let's get the other horses all ready for the ride." Lord Wallace headed back to the stable yard and proceeded to check the tack of all the horses that were waiting in their stables.

The other students soon appeared, and there was much excited chatter as they got their horses out of the stables and secured various bags and bedding rolls to the saddles. Then they all mounted up, with more rucksacks secured on their own backs.

Carlotta was joining them for the first time on this ride. Nobody dared to say anything to her as they knew this was an important moment and they didn't want to put her off. But as she mounted up on Duchess and lightly settled into the saddle, Xinia gave her a secret smile. She was so pleased to see Carlotta on a horse after all her fears and worries.

"Why don't you ride with me?" Xinia invited. Carlotta smiled gratefully. She knew that Xinia was an outstanding horsewoman, and it would give her confidence to have her by her side.

"Yes, please," replied Carlotta. "It would really help."

Xinia nodded and decided to stay very close to Carlotta all day. Now they had her riding again after everything that had happened, Xinia didn't want anything to go wrong or for Carlotta to lose confidence.

Sergeant Yeald noted the interaction between the two girls and smiled with satisfaction to see the students rallying to support Carlotta as well as guard her.

"I can't wait to see inside the cave again," said Lucy, as they were riding out up the track. "I want a closer look at those blue crystals!"

"I am looking forward to getting everything set up in there to make a hideaway," declared Mark. "We will make it fit for a King!"

Lord Wallace chuckled. If only they knew who sometimes walked these mountains!

The ride progressed up the mountain, the track weaving and winding around the mountainside, giving splendid views of the Loch. The early morning sun glanced off the water, and the surface glittered with golden reflections through the morning mist.

"Oh my goodness!" exclaimed Carlotta. "That is so beautiful! I am glad I came out with you all today."

"We are glad you came with us," said Xinia softly. "Isn't this just the best way to see the countryside?"

Duchess gave a friendly long snort.

"She thinks so!" called Charlie, with a giggle.

Carlotta smiled at her horse. She and Duchess had come to a fine understanding now, and she wasn't alarmed by the noise Duchess made. She knew Duchess was just expressing herself – either that or blowing the stable dust out of her nostrils. Carlotta wasn't sure which, but she knew Duchess was very relaxed and it made her feel relaxed too.

The students were riding out much earlier in the day than they had on their previous outing. So the views were quite different from before. The morning mist and the early morning sun conspired to show them new landscape views, new colours and new light.

199

As the horses steadily walked them higher and higher, the students grew quiet, transfixed by the beauty all around them. The mountains were so magnificent; nobody had words big enough to describe or exclaim about them. So they just looked and recorded what they saw to the cameras of their own memory. They all knew they would want to remember this day and the loveliness they had seen.

Eventually, they arrived at the Blue Caves. This woke the students up somewhat, and suddenly everyone was very excited.

"Now, before you go into the caves and start setting up, I want to show you how to keep your horses safe in an environment like this," said Sensei Tanaka. "This is a useful Ninja skill that you should know, and today is the perfect time to learn it!"

Sensei Tanaka hopped off his horse and untied long ropes that were coiled and attached either side of the back of the saddle. Handing his reins to Sergeant Yeald, he then proceeded to teach the students how to build a temporary corral for the horses by winding the rope around nearby trees. When they were finished, there was a surprisingly effective ring of rope held firmly in place by the trees. They had made a paddock for the horses amongst the trees.

"This is far from being very secure and is not the ideal way to keep a horse safe for very long, but if you are outdoors and there are no better alternatives, it can be an option. If a horse is scared, he will escape from many enclosures if he wants to. He will escape from this very easily. But most of the time, this will be fine. It just lets your horse know this is where you would like him to stay. Horses are very helpful people and will normally try to work with you. It is certainly nicer for a horse to be left in a corral than it is to be left tied to a tree and unable to graze."

"Before we put our horses in the corral, I have a question for you: What if your horses get upset whilst they are in there?" Sensei Tanaka asked the students, testing them a little now.

Charlie's hand went straight up to answer. "Will they break out?"

Sensei Tanaka nodded. "What do you think?"

Xinia spoke up. "Yes, I think they will, Sensei. We will need to calm them before they get to that point."

Sensei Tanaka looked around at the students. "Xinia has told you something here that you might not realise because you haven't been training with horses very long. But Xinia knows this because she has had a horse of her own a long time. The lesson is this: if you can calm a horse when he first becomes a little anxious about something, you can very often prevent him becoming very worried or doing something big or dangerous to express his fear. Always look for the little signs that tell you your horse is becoming anxious. A great horseman or horsewoman can read the tiniest of expressions and know what the horse is feeling. And an even greater one can then calm the horse and make him feel more comfortable.

"So what will our plan be here? With horses and as a warrior, you must always have a plan. Whilst you always hope for and visualise the best, you must also consider what can go wrong. Then you can take precautions and make a plan for that situation."

He pointed to Mark. "What's your plan?"

Mark looked at the horses, the corral and the cave and thought a moment. "What if we put one person watching the horses and another at the mouth of the cave? Then if the horses get at all distressed, the person watching the horses will signal to another person watching at the mouth to the caves and then we can all come out immediately and go to our horses?"

Sensei Tanaka gave him a broad smile. "Excellent thinking, Mark! That's an excellent plan! Do we have a volunteer to stay with the horses?"

Xinia raised her hand. As the best horsewoman amongst them, she was best skilled to stay with the horses. She knew she could read the horse's mood and feelings better than any of them.

David raised his hand next. "I will stand guard at the mouth to the cave Sensei. I have already been inside it, so I am happy to let the others go in instead."

With this plan in place, they took all the equipment they had brought up the mountain and placed it in a pile and then took their horses into the corral, where Xinia supervised them with Sensei Tanaka looking on.

"I think that we should leave the corral ropes up here in the cave, so they are here if you should ever need them," suggested Sensei Tanaka.

Xinia nodded. "I think so too."

Mark was very keen to supervise the organisation of the

supplies and kit. He felt in charge of this operation because it had been his idea. So he happily went around organising the carrying of equipment into the cave and telling all the other students where to put things.

"Now make sure everything is waterproof and protected from the wildlife! Let's make sure those food tins are securely closed! And make sure the bedding is all wrapped and covered in tarpaulins!"

The other students didn't mind Mark taking charge. They knew he liked to do it and would be happiest if he felt sure that everything had been set up well.

Carlotta was very interested to see inside the cave. She hadn't been on the previous visit here and had only heard about the blue crystals. Hearing about them didn't prepare her for their beauty, though. She gasped as Lucy shone a torch on a rich seam of blue crystals at the back of the cave.

"Aren't they gorgeous?" Lucy asked Carlotta.

Carlotta nodded vigorously. "They are incredible! Wow! I would love to chip a bit off and wear it as a necklace!"

"We had better not," replied Lucy. "But we could ask Lord Wallace about it. Maybe there are some crystals somewhere that we could take home. I know my mother would love to see one. She loves pretty, natural things."

Chapter 29

When they got back from the expedition to the Blue Caves, the students helped untack their horses and then went off to explore the castle grounds before dark. Only Mark stayed behind at the stables. He had taken Lord Wallace's invitation to help train Zeebee very seriously and was determined to get started on it.

Mark went to Zeebee's paddock to see him. Little Stumpy, the Shetland Pony, came straight over to investigate Mark, with high hopes of treats. When he realised Mark didn't have anything for him, he nudged his leg sharply to register his displeasure and wandered off in search of the tastiest patch of grass.

Zeebee watched this from a distance. He grazed steadily, his eye constantly on Mark. From time to time, he looked up at him for a moment before dropping his head again. Mark remembered what Lord Wallace had told him. So he turned his back on Zeebee and rested his arms on the fence. He was doing his level best to ignore Zeebee whilst trying to work out where he was and what he might be doing.

At first, it was impossible, and Mark felt impatient. But he was a very determined boy who was not likely to give in.

So he made a game of it. He held onto the fence and closed his eyes. He started listening really hard, straining his ears to hear Zeebee's feet move as he grazed and the gentle chomping sound Zeebee made when he chewed grass.

Mark found himself holding his breath so he could hear better without the sound of his own breathing competing with the small sounds he was listening for. He soon realised that he wouldn't be able to hold his breath for long. So he started taking very slow, controlled breaths. He found that his ears could separate the sounds of his breaths then from the sounds he was listening for. Mark found this an interesting experience. He hadn't realised how important listening and careful breathing could be before. He decided that this was a very useful Ninja skill. If he can hear a horse grazing behind him, he could also hear a potential attacker creeping up on him. He made a mental note to discuss this with Sensei Tanaka and tell the other students about it. He smiled, very pleased with himself for making this discovery.

Zeebee watched the boy at the fence. He experimented with grazing a little closer, but Zeebee was in no hurry to take any chances. It was getting dark by the time Mark decided it was time to stop for the day. He was disappointed that Zeebee hadn't come to him in the several hours that he had stood there. But Lord Wallace had warned him that it would take time. He allowed himself a brief look at Zeebee before climbing out of the paddock. Zeebee made a little squeal of protest and arched his neck as he sprang away. Mark was annoyed with himself. He knew it would have been better if he had just slipped quietly out of the paddock. But he couldn't resist taking a look at Zeebee and had done so. He had paid for his mistake. As he walked back to the castle for dinner, he hoped it was a mistake he could recover from.

Sensei Tanaka was very interested to hear about Mark's experience with the horse, when Mark told him about it after dinner. "Excellent!" he said. "Your horse is teaching you a very valuable Ninja skill, the ability to listen. Accept this lesson and take all you can from it! Listen well and learn to visualise the world as you hear it. If you do this well, you will be able to anticipate incoming attacks that you can't see. It's a very powerful ability to develop. Excellent, Mark! I look forward to hearing more!"

Feeling buoyed by this, Mark went and discussed Zeebee's reaction to him at the end of the session today with Lord Wallace.

"Never mind, young Mark. These things happen. It isn't terrible. He was just telling you he felt under pressure and didn't like it."

"He felt under pressure because I looked at him?" asked Mark in amazement.

"Well, if someone looked at you, you might feel under pressure, mightn't you?" Lord Wallace explained.

"I don't think so, Sir," replied Mark. "People look at me all the time, and I don't mind."

"But how would you feel if you were a prey animal and a predator was looking at you? Might that worry you?"

"But I'm not going to eat him!" protested Mark.

"He doesn't know that. Someone hurt him once, and now he worries that other humans might. It's your job to help him understand that most people are pretty decent and won't hurt him."

Mark began to understand what Lord Wallace was saying. He resolved to be more careful about where he looked in future.

Mark went to see Zeebee at every opportunity that arose. He ran down to the stables before breakfast, in between lessons, in the time between lunch and the afternoon lessons and then before dinner. Some days he got up early to get more time in with Zeebee. On such days, he rose with the sun and was rewarded with the sight of the beautiful morning mist as it floated across the Highland countryside.

One such morning, he went down to the paddock where Zeebee was and found it covered in such thick mist that he couldn't see the horses. But he waited patiently by the fence anyway. Gradually, out of the mist, a figure appeared. At first, he could only make out two long pointed ears. The figure became more distinct as it drew closer. Mark kept his head tilted down. He breathed slowly and carefully turned his back to the horse. The was the first time Zeebee had chosen to walk up to him, and he didn't want to alarm him as he had done previously. So he stood by the fence, closed his eyes and listened with all his might. The sounds created a picture inside his mind, and he became aware of the horse drawing closer and closer. Then he felt warm breath on his hand. He froze. He thought that if a look can spook a horse, then a movement at such time was likely to cause greater alarm. So he remained motionless and his senses focussed on the warm breathing of the horse on his hand and then the soft touch of his muzzle. Mark smiled. As the horse made gentle contact, his heart felt full of joy and light.

They stayed like this, boy and horse, for what felt like an age. Eventually, Mark knew that he would be late for classes if he didn't leave. So he carefully moved away from the horse and climbed quietly through the fence without looking at him. But he felt the connection he had experienced with Zeebee throughout the rest of the day.

Chapter 30

Lord Wallace was delighted to see Mark's progress with Zeebee. After that day of first contact, a growing trust and confidence had developed between the boy and horse. Zeebee gradually allowed Mark more contact. Mark followed Lord Wallace's advice and always let Zeebee come to him rather than attempt to approach him himself. He found that Zeebee became increasingly confident with him and, after a while, he could stroke Zeebee's neck and smooth his long fluffy mane.

The sessions always started the same, with Mark standing at the fence with his back to the horse and listening for his approach. Mark found that his sense of hearing was developing beyond anything he could have imagined. He began to develop a second form of vision from the rich tapestry of sounds from around the meadows. Some times he thought he heard the faint rustle and footsteps of another human. He heard sounds from the woodland at the far end of the paddock. Mark felt watched – and not for the first time. He had become aware of this feeling whilst at the Academy, and it was here now too. When he thought about it, he had felt watched for a long time, before the Academy even. He was a sensible boy though and assumed that this was how everyone felt. There were so many people around most of the time, after all.

He felt a nudge at his elbow as Zeebee announced his arrival. Mark grinned and turned quietly. "Hello boy," he said softly and rubbed Zeebee's neck. Zeebee arched his neck and sniffed at Mark's pockets.

"Oh, you want something, do you?" Mark chuckled as Zeebee put his nose against Mark's jacket and tossed it open. "I'll see what I can find for you."

Mark slipped away from him and went in search of some horse feed to give him. He filled his pocket from a metal bin in the feed shed and returned to find Zeebee waiting for him at the fence.

"Well, Lord Wallace did say that I was to help teach you that people can be nice, so I think this will be okay." Mark climbed through the fence and offered a little grain to Zeebee on the palm of his hand. Zeebee sniffed the offering and then whiffled his lips over the grain experimentally. He was pleased with what he found there and accepted the treat with pleasure.

"You like that, do you?" asked Mark. "Let's see if there is

any more in my pocket, shall we?"

When all the grain had been offered and accepted, Mark stood stroking Zeebee and talking to him. He told him what a lovely horse he was and how we wished he could be his horse. Zeebee listened intently to every word that he said.

Zeebee looked up suddenly. Lord Wallace was on his way over and was carrying a grooming brush. "I see you two are getting on rather well. I thought you might give him a brush."

Mark quietly reached for the brush. He was about to put it to Zeebee's neck when Lord Wallace advised, "Let him sniff it first. He will feel better about it if he takes a look at it before you touch him with it."

Mark did as Lord Wallace suggested. Zeebee sniffed the brush a moment before losing interest in it. Mark looked to Lord Wallace, who smiled and nodded to him.

"I think he has told you it's fine."

Mark started brushing Zeebee's mane and shoulder and gradually worked along his back. He sensed a tension as he moved away from Zeebee's head. His instinct was to pull back from anything that made Zeebee feel less comfortable, so he moved back to brushing his neck and shoulder. Lord Wallace nodded approvingly. "That's right. Let him tell you what he is comfortable with. He will allow more in time, but he needs to gain confidence that you won't push him further than he is happy to go. You have a good sense of this, Mark. Listen to your instincts and try and focus on what he is feeling. Eventually, you may be able to sense his feelings as if they were your own."

Mark looked at Lord Wallace. He was sure that this man had a great understanding of horses, but what he was saying sounded impossible. However, Mark was learning that things that seem impossible very often are not.

Lord Wallace had one more piece of advice for Mark. "Now make sure you leave Zeebee on a good note, whilst he is happy and relaxed. You want him to remember his time with you as a good thing. Never be tempted to push him to the point of refusal or discomfort. A great skill in horsemanship is knowing when to stop the lesson."

"I think this would be a good time then, Sir," decided Mark. "He is happy, and we have made progress since yesterday."

"Well judged!" praised Lord Wallace. "And tomorrow is another day."

Chapter 31

When Mark told the other students about how he had learned to see with his hearing, they were all very interested. They decided to ask Sensei Goodwin about it during their martial arts lesson.

"Ah! I knew you would be asking me this one day, but I wasn't expecting it yet!" Sensei Goodwin was surprised and pleased. "It is quite an advanced ability that you are asking about. It seems Mark has stumbled upon it by accident. But it is a very valuable skill to have, and it won't do any harm to start learning it now if you are keen."

"Yes please, Sensei!" they all chorused.

"Very well. Here is a very simple exercise we can do to help you learn this. I will demonstrate. Can I have a volunteer to be uke?"

Charlie's hand shot up first. Sensei Goodwin laughed. "Always first, Charlie! Your bravery is commendable!"

"Now I am going to stand over here with my back to you, and I want you to walk up behind me and tap me on the shoulder, please."

Sensei Goodwin took up his position and Charlie did as he was bid. He walked up behind Sensei Goodwin and reached out to tap him in his left shoulder. As he did so, Sensei Goodwin's left arm went up.

"Again!" called the Sensei.

Charlie walked back to his original position. This time he approached a little faster and attempted to tap Sensei Goodwin on the right shoulder. Before he could, Sensei Goodwin's right arm went up.

Sensei Goodwin turned and made a slight bow to Charlie, who bowed in return. "Thank you, Charlie."

"Do you see? This is a very simple exercise to start with, but it requires you to develop a sense of where an incoming attacker might be and what direction he is approaching from. Initially, it is enough to know when he is close, though. It will be easier if we do this one at a time as it involves listening very carefully."

One by one, the students took it in turns to stand with their back to the class as one of the other students approached them. Hands went up as they sensed the approach. Some of the students did better than others, but as the class went on, and they had more opportunities to try, they found they got better.

"Very good! You are getting the idea of it. You just need to practise now. I suggest you practise this amongst yourselves both indoors and outdoors. Sound behaves differently in different environments so you should vary your practise." Sensei Goodwin was pleased with their first attempts. "Now assuming you have learned to sense an incoming attack, what are you going to do about it?"

Gina's hand went up. "Block it, Sensei?"

"Yes, that's one option," said Sensei Goodwin. "Any other options?" he looked around the room at the students, who were racking their brains for ideas.

Charlie put his hand up. "Hit them, Sensei?"

"Well, yes, but we try to be a bit more sophisticated and peaceful than that if we can," chuckled Sensei Goodwin.

Mark remembered a time on the Assessment Course when Sensei Goodwin had done a dramatic demonstration that involved stepping out of the way of a tumbling boulder. He put his hand up to answer. "Step out of the way, Sensei?"

"Very good Mark! That is an excellent option. There is another option that we seek to deploy. I don't think you will think of it though."

Lucy put her hand up shyly. "Could we make their energy go somewhere else, Sensei?"

Sensei Goodwin was very pleasantly surprised. "Goodness! I didn't expect that. Yes, Lucy. You can redirect their energy. That may be a little advanced for you all at this point, but I am delighted that you are thinking in those terms already. Well done!

"Right then. Let's explore some of those options, shall we? Let's start with the block." Sensei Goodwin went on to demonstrate how to turn and block the incoming attack when they sensed it. The students all took their turn in trying this.

"Let's try the stepping out of the way option that Mark suggested shall we?" Sensei Goodwin demonstrated a very elegant swivel away from the incoming attack at the last moment. The students were very impressed and did their best to copy him when it was their turn.

"Again, this is something you can practise amongst

yourselves. If you do it really well next lesson, I will let you try it wearing blindfolds! But don't try it with blindfolds until we practise it in class. I don't want any accidents! I know how keen you all are!"

Chapter 32

Xinia and Pandora's mother, Anna Black, was annoyed. She had been summoned to Superintendent Michael's office after her shift. She had been riding the streets of London on her big black police horse, Gabriel, all afternoon and she had been looking forward to putting her feet up and having a cup of tea before going home. As she untacked Gabriel and gave him his usual post-ride back rub, she tried not to let her thoughts about Superintendent Michael go through her fingers into the horse. She thoroughly disliked the Superintendent, and the last thing she wanted to do right now was go and talk to him. But orders were orders, and she had no choice in the matter.

Gabriel knew Anna very well after all these years working together. He could tell she had become unhappy since getting back to the stables. As she was leaving his stall, he rubbed his big head against her in solidarity.

"Oh Gabriel! If only people were as nice as you are!" Anna rubbed Gabriel's forehead before planting a kiss on his big black velvet muzzle. "Good boy. Thank you for looking after me again today." She ran her hand down his powerful neck. Unable to resist, she gave his neck a big hug and felt his great strength and power energise her. "Thank you for that too."

Reluctantly, she left her horse to eat his hay and made her way to Superintendent Michael's office.

Anna paused at the door a moment to gather her self control and compose her face. She knew that it was best not to let this man know how much she disliked him. That involved arranging her face into a convincing smile. It was always an effort to remember to do that, though. Anna was much more used to being honest about her feelings. She loved the way she could be like that with horses but knew that it wasn't always possible with humans.

"Come in! Come in!" Superintendent Michael beckoned her in. His face was plastered with an even less convincing smile than Anna's. She was immediately suspicious. He only pretended to be nice when he wanted something. He didn't do a very good job of pretending to be nice of course, but it was a marked contrast to his more usual attitude which was even less charming, if such a thing could be imagined.

"Take a seat!" he invited with similarly fake friendliness. She did as she was bid, although she was far from relaxed as she sat. She had the distinct impression she had walked into a trap of some sort.

"How are you getting along with that horse? Gabriel, is it?" he asked lightly.

Anna was immediately concerned. If he was asking about Gabriel, he might be planning to separate her from her horse partner. He had the power to do that and was nasty enough to do so if it either served his purpose or amused his sadistic mind. Anna decided that a detached, professional response was safest. "He is working very well with me, Sir. No problems at all."

"Good! Good!" Superintendent Michael was searching for another subject to lead the conversation where he privately intended. "And how is young Pandora getting on at her new school? Is that working out?"

Superintendent Michael had been instrumental in getting Pandora a place at Shadowlands when she had failed the Assessment Course at The Academy. So Anna had little choice but to give his question a polite answer. "Very well, Sir. We hardly hear from her, but the headmaster tells us she is doing very well and excelling at languages."

"Excellent! And how about Xinia? Is she enjoying the

Academy?" he crept carefully into this part of the conversation. Anna didn't spot his particular interest, unfortunately.

"She is doing very well, thank you. She is away on a field trip at the moment, but she will be back at the end of term."

"Oh yes?" Superintendent Michael almost held his breath, desperate to get a very particular piece of information from her. "Where did she go?"

"The Scottish Highlands. Apparently, it is very beautiful there, so I am sure she is having a lovely time." Anna unwittingly had given Superintendent Michael precisely what he wanted. He puffed up in excitement, keen to get her out of his office now that he had the information he needed.

"Jolly good! Well, I hope she has an interesting time there. I am sure she will." He gave Anna a deeply insincere smile. "Well, thank you for this little chat. I have another meeting now, so you are dismissed."

As she left his office, Anna felt uneasy. He had asked her about her horse and her daughters and then pretty much had thrown her out of his office. It was strange behaviour even by his standards.

Chapter 33

The headmaster of Shadowlands wore a wide smirk on his face when he put the phone down. He was very pleased with the information he had just received from Superintendent Michael. He agreed with the Superintendent. If the Academy had taken the girl to Scotland - and his sources told him that the entire first year was missing from the Academy - then it was almost certain that they would have gone to Wallace's place.

Shadowlands made it their business to know as much as possible about everyone who passed through the Academy and kept extensive files on each of them. The only Academy contact who could accommodate the entire group of first years in the Scottish Highlands was Wallace. He was also aware that Wallace's two sons were in the first year at the Academy too. It all added up. That's where they must have taken the girl.

With this information churning in his head, he summoned Instructor Adams to his office. A student was sent to track down Instructor Adams, who was tormenting his class of first-years on the training ground.

When Adams appeared in the headmaster's office, he was

told the news. "I know exactly where they have taken her! And just in time! The last vote for the Fairweather Bill is on Christmas Eve. So we need to capture his daughter before then. We only have a few days to get this organised. We need to arrange facilities and transport, get a team up to Scotland and launch an attack on Kaey Castle to take the girl before Christmas Eve. No mess-ups this time! Take that Pandora with you so she can identify the girl and tell her apart from her sister. I don't want you making the same mistake again and bringing back the sister!"

Instructor Adams' eyes glittered. The mention of their previous failure angered him, but he relished the opportunity to lead an operation to put right what they got wrong last time. He set his jaw in a determined expression. "Leave it with me, Sir. It will be done."

Instructor Adams marched back to his class, which he had left doing sit-ups on the training ground. "Right! Get up you lot! There is no time to waste. Get back to your huts. I want you showered, changed and packed for a mission before dinner. Then you are going to have an early night and be up early in the morning, ready to leave. Tomorrow we are going on a mission to kidnap the girl again."

The students exchanged surprised glances. Pandora

chuckled. "Are we going to take my sister again?" she asked with mock innocence.

Instructor Adams shot her a glance of pure poison. "No, you are not. There will be absolutely no mistakes. Pandora, I will hold you personally responsible if we don't get the right girl. You are going to make it your business to make absolutely sure that it is Carlotta Fairweather that we kidnap this time!"

Pandora knew better than to risk angering him further. She had got off quite lightly by joking about kidnapping her sister again. She knew it was a sore point. Fortunately, Instructor Adams was more interested in planning the next operation to give her any further attention.

The headmaster watched all this from his office window. He picked up the phone and made a call.

"We are going after her again. We know where they have taken her. She will be in our care by Christmas Eve." There was a pause as the voice on the other end spoke. Then the headmaster replied. "Absolutely, Ma'am. No mistakes this time. It will be done."

When he put the phone down, he continued to look out of

the window thoughtfully. This was a crucial moment for him, for Shadowlands, for the entire organisation and the country itself. He took a deep breath as he considered his role in the history that was about to unfold. To think that his school, his team, his people were going to be the force that prevented the abominable Free Speech Bill from entering British law! They would be responsible for bringing an entire country under subtle control and preparing them for the New Order. What changes would be possible if speech could be controlled! The organisation, of which he was a small but significant part, had grand plans for the future. The country would become unrecognisable! Without the freedom to express a dissenting view, the ordinary people of the country would be powerless to stand in the way of progress. What progress there would be!

The headmaster pondered his own future. What rewards and recognition must surely follow for him! He wondered what position he would be given in the future, whether there would be impressive titles and powers. He felt certain that the organisation would reward him and acknowledge the significant part he was about to play.

He continued to gaze out of the window. But he no longer saw the training grounds. He saw his future and the future of the entire country stretching out in front of him.

Chapter 34

The students were getting excited about Christmas, although they were sad that they wouldn't be going home to their families for it.

Lord Wallace spoke to them about it after dinner, a few days before Christmas. "We had hoped you would be able to get back to your families for Christmas, of course. But with her father's Bill going to the final vote on Christmas Eve, we have to keep Carlotta safe here until then."

The students nodded and agreed. They understood. The whole point of coming to Scotland was to protect Carlotta, and this was the final part of the operation. Still, it was hard to give up on having Christmas.

Lady Wallace sensed how they felt. "You poor wee things! Don't worry. We will make this a Christmas to remember! You might be stuck up here and away from your families, but let's make this special! We have a few days left, so if your Senseis allow it, you can help us decorate the castle and prepare for a great feast on Christmas Eve! We can celebrate both Christmas and the end of a job well done. Will you help me get everything ready?"

Everyone's face lit up. This sounded exciting! "May we?" the students all appealed to Sensei Goodwin and Sensei Tanaka. They smiled and agreed.

"Just don't forget what you are here for though," warned Sensei Goodwin. "By all means have fun, but remember that Carlotta is in danger until that final vote is complete down in London."

Sensei Tanaka agreed. "It is still more than possible that Shadowlands will come after her here. You must remember everything you have been taught about situational awareness. You must be watching out every moment of every day. Whatever you do, wherever you go, you must be watching and listening. You must know where Carlotta is at all times and always be thinking about how to get her to safety."

Sergeant Yeald nodded in agreement. "Yes, the threat level is still high. You will still need everything you have been taught about bodyguarding in these last few days before Christmas."

Mark put his hand up. "Would it help if we organised ourselves to sleep in shifts so that there is always someone watching out at night?"

Sergeant Yeald was very pleased with this suggestion. "Excellent plan, Mark. Exactly that. Take every precaution!"

"If that's all settled, who is going to help me make a start on the decorations?" Lady Wallace asked with a warm smile. A dozen hands shot up.

"Wonderful! Come along with me then. Let's go and find the boxes of decorations and see what we can do to make the castle ready for Christmas!"

With that, she bustled off to a remote room in the castle with a train of eager and excited students following behind her. They were amazed to find that an entire room had been dedicated to accommodating boxes and boxes of Christmas decorations.

Lucy opened a box of Christmas tree ornaments. She took one out, unwrapped it from the sheet of newspaper that protected it and held it up to the light. It glittered and sparkled as the light passed through the glass bauble and reflected off the silver glitter patterns that adorned it.

"Wow! That's pretty!" she exclaimed. "Lady Wallace, where will the Christmas tree go?"

"Ah! Well, we have enough decorations for a few trees. We will have one in the main hall, one in the dining room and a great big one out in the courtyard. I do love to see an outdoor tree as well as an indoor one, don't you?"

Lucy laughed. She had never seen an outdoor Christmas tree before. "That sounds magical!"

Charlie popped up from behind a pile of boxes, wearing a silver garland around his neck and another coiled on his head as a glittery hat. "I could sit on top of the tree!" He grinned, and everyone laughed.

With the same organisation and sense of purpose with which they had equipped the Blue Cave, the students worked together in the days that followed to thoroughly decorate the castle. Every staircase was wound with sparkling garlands; they made chains out of shiny paper to string across the ceilings and along every wall. Lord Wallace led expeditions outdoors to collect holly, mistletoe and various boughs of greenery with which to add further decoration. Holly wreaths were tied, and centrepieces for the Christmas table were made.

Lord Wallace had selected a large Spruce tree for the courtyard. The students were amazed to see him bring it back in from the forest with the help of Samson, the large draft horse who had been carrying Sergeant Yeald during his stay at the castle. Samson was wearing a heavy collar around his neck to which was attached a simple metal contraption which attached to the base of the tree and dragged it all the way into the courtyard. Lord Wallace was guiding Samson from his hindquarters with a set of very long reins that attached to his head collar.

"This is so much better than using a tractor," explained Lord Wallace. "Samson here will only leave a few footprints in the forest. His feet won't plough up the ground in the way that a tractor would. And he likes playing his part in the Christmas preparations, don't you old boy?" he rubbed Samson's shoulder appreciatively. Samson gave a contented long snort.

After Samson had been returned to the herd in the top fields, Lord Wallace then proceeded to plant the tree in what looked like a well in the middle of the courtyard. It wasn't a well at all, just a round flowerbed type structure built with the same stone as the rest of the castle. The tree was very big and heavy, so Lord Wallace used a system of ropes and pulleys to pull the tree into place before securing it with metal bands and straps within the well. Then he brought in bags of compost to fill around the base of the tree. The students helped him cover up the roots with the compost and then water it from a hosepipe. "There, that should keep him safe and happy! We can plant him back out in the New Year."

"You replant the tree, Sir?" Mark thought this was an interesting idea.

"Oh yes! In fact, this isn't the first time this tree has come in for our Christmas celebrations. We always dig them up and then replant them after Christmas. I hate to see a plant or tree die when we can give it a new life. This one is getting a bit big to dig up though, so I think it will be his last Christmas in here. He will be just as happy in the forest, though."

Nell looked a bit sad. She felt sorry for the tree. "So is his Christmas destiny over, Sir?"

Lord Wallace smiled. "Destiny takes many forms. Who knows what it will hold for any of us? But yes, it is likely that it is his destiny to be a tree who just lives in a forest in future. But that's okay. It's what trees are meant to do."

"Can we decorate it now please, Sir?" Charlie was excited

at the thought of decorating an outdoor Christmas Tree. He had never seen one before and was very keen.

"Oh, I think we have done enough for today. Decorating this is a big job and will take all day. We have one more day tomorrow before Christmas Eve, so let's do it then."

The students agreed that this would be the best plan. They went in for dinner and afterwards went up to their bedrooms in the turret, full of chatter and excitement. Despite this, Mark insisted on organising the sentry detail for the night.

"I'll take the first Watch," he decided.

"I'll join you," said Charlie companionably.

"Then Xinia and I will take the next Watch," offered Lucy.

"We will do the early morning shift," agreed James and Malcolm.

Carlotta smiled shyly. "Thank you, everyone. I can't tell you how much this all means to me. I am so grateful, truly. Hopefully, it will all be over soon."

She looked a little sad. "I am going to miss you all so

much."

"Can't you stay?" asked Mark.

"I don't think they would have me. I am not a real Academy student, after all. They just took me in to look after me. But once my Father's Bill is passed, there won't be a need anymore. I will have to go back to living at home in London with my Father and having tutors," Carlotta explained regretfully.

"But maybe if you ask they will let you stay?" Lucy suggested.

"You never know unless you ask!" exclaimed Charlie. "It's worth a try."

"You can't just go back to your old life," said Xinia. "Not after all you have gone through. Now you have martial arts and horses and friends!"

"I will ask, but I think it is hopeless. My Father will want me back where he can see me. And I am not good enough for the Academy. You all went on a selection course and were chosen. They didn't choose me." Carlotta was resigned. She understood her situation perfectly well.

"I bet they would have chosen you if you had been on the selection course though," said Mark, loyally.

"Yes!" all the students agree with Mark.

"That's very kind of you, but I don't think so," Carlotta shook her head.

"But you will ask, won't you?" Lucy pressed her.

Carlotta smiled at her. "Yes, I will ask."

"Right then, you lot had better get to bed and Charlie and I will start our first Watch shift." Mark was back into organising mode.

Chapter 35

The next day was a flurry of excitement as the students worked to dress the big tree in the courtyard. They draped it in coloured garlands, hung shiny ornaments from it, and Lord Wallace taught them how to tie candles onto the branches in such a way that they would be held securely and not set fire to the tree.

"I can't wait to light these!" cried Lucy. "It is going to look so pretty!"

"It will be simply beautiful," said Carlotta dreamily, imagining how the tree would look when they were finished, and the candles lit.

They completed the decorations just before darkness fell. Lady Wallace brought them mugs of steaming hot fruit punch, spiced with cloves and cinnamon. "To ward off the cold!" she explained.

The boys and girls gratefully sipped at the sweet, warm drink, warming their hands on the mugs and looking up at the tree. Each one of them visualised how it would look tomorrow night when they lit the candles on Christmas Eve.

Mark took his mug of punch down to the stables so he could drink it whilst talking to Zeebee. "It's going to be a magical Christmas boy!" he whispered to him, stroking his forehead with one hand and holding his steaming mug in the other. Zeebee sniffed at the mug.

"Oh no, that's too hot, and I don't know if you are allowed it. But I brought you a carrot. Would that do instead?" Mark fished in his pockets and pulled out a long thin carrot that he had begged from the cook earlier.

Mark chattered away to Zeebee, telling him all about Christmas. "I've never had Christmas in a castle before! I will miss my Mum, though. But don't tell anyone. They might think I'm soft." Zeebee nuzzled him. "Yes, I know you are a big softy! I am so glad we are friends now."

Duchess wandered over to see if there might be a carrot for her too. Stumpy had been sent back to the main herd in disgrace after rolling under the fencing rails one too many times, escaping and making his way into the castle kitchen. Cook had been horrified to find a plump Shetland pony helping himself to her vegetables and had banished him. So Duchess had been brought down from the top fields to keep Zeebee company. She nuzzled Mark's pocket and was delighted to be rewarded with a carrot of her own. "I brought supplies!" laughed Mark.

Suddenly, Zeebee threw his head up and stared towards the castle courtyard. He braced his legs and seemed to shake with alarm. Duchess looked up too. Her ears were pricked and eyes fixed on the same point as Zeebee's. Something was wrong! Mark knew that Zeebee was prone to alarm, but if Duchess was concerned too, there must be a problem. Putting his mug down, he went into stealth mode, using all the Ninja Stealth that Sensei Tanaka had taught them.

Careful to stay in the shadows, Mark crept along the edge of the stable block, then dropped and crawled to the castle wall before slinking along in the shadows of the wall towards the entrance to the courtyard, all the way avoiding presenting a silhouette against the bright moonlit sky. As he approached, he could hear shouting and crashing. It sounded like a fight – a big fight with a lot of people.

Careful to make sure that nobody saw him, he peered around the corner to see what was happening. He opened his eyes in amazement. The courtyard was full of battling ninjas! All his school friends were there – and Sergeant Yeald. But there were about thirty strange ninjas, dressed in black with their faces covered, attacking them. Carlotta was near the centre of the courtyard by the Christmas tree and was holding her own, fighting fiercely with the rest of them. Mark could see his friends were using all the martial arts techniques they had been taught. They were blocking, evading, pivoting and sending their attackers flying. His first instinct was to run in and join the fight. But he knew what his job was now. He was now the chief bodyguard, and it was up to him to get the Principal away rather than get involved in the fighting. This was the moment he had been trained for. He ran back to the stables, grabbed a head-collar with reins and put it on Duchess.

"Sorry boy, you aren't ready for this," he apologised to Zeebee. He knew Duchess could do what was needed now, though. Remembering how Sensei Tanaka had taught them to mount from the ground, he swung himself up onto Duchess.

"I need your help now girl. Please!"

Duchess knew what was needed. She knew too that Mark had no saddle to keep him secure on her back. So she carried him with great care as he urged her to the castle courtyard.

Entering the courtyard at a fast trot, Mark made straight for

244

Carlotta. Sergeant Yeald was roaring. He had been set upon by a dozen ninjas, some of them powerful adults. He had been trying to rid himself of them so he could take Carlotta away, but the Shadowlands ninjas had made a special plan to target him in particular and had brought in some special ninja operatives to do so. They reasoned that, if they could incapacitate him, it would be a simple matter to then take the girl.

"Carlotta!" Mark cried as he pushed Duchess on through the fighting ninjas towards her. Carlotta climbed up onto the well and as Mark passed, he extended an arm to her and swept her up behind him on Duchess.

"Go!" yelled Sergeant Yeald.

Mark knew where. This is what they had prepared for. He clamped his legs onto Duchess and repeated what Sergeant Yeald had said to her. "Go!" he yelled.

Duchess needed no further encouragement. She knew what to do and even where to go. She set off out of the courtyard at a canter, with Mark and Carlotta clinging to her.

Mark was grateful for the bright moonlight which lit their path as they cantered up the mountain. Duchess knew the track so well, she could probably have navigated it in the dark, but the moonlight certainly helped, and it gave Mark and Carlotta confidence that they were heading in the right direction.

Chapter 36

Pandora had seen Mark and Carlotta make their escape on Duchess. She was caught up in the battle at the time, and it was a little while before she could break away. But when she did, Pandora ran out of the castle courtyard and went in search of the stables.

Running along the line of stables, she checked each of them, looking for a horse to take so she could ride in pursuit of Mark and Carlotta. To her annoyance, every stable was empty. All the horses had been taken to the top fields for some horse time, away from mankind and the castle. Lord Wallace liked to do this regularly so that the horses had a more natural and enjoyable life. On this occasion, it was a matter of great inconvenience to Pandora, though. She couldn't believe that there wasn't a single horse in this large stable yard!

She heard outraged whinnies and calls coming from a small paddock behind the stables. She found Zeebee there, pacing up and down the fence line calling out. He didn't like being left on his own at all!

Pandora smiled. This was exactly what she needed. She sized him up and decided that a cob sized bridle would suit him. Then she went in search of the tack room. She was a bit confused to find that the tack room only seemed to contain saddles and head-collars with reins attached to them. Didn't these people use proper bridles? How on earth where you meant to control a horse without a bit in his mouth? Clearly, these people had some strange ideas. Nevertheless, if this is what the horses were used to, this is what she needed. She grabbed one that looked about the right size and had the foresight to also fill her pockets with grain to catch the horse.

When he realised she had grain for him, Zeebee stopped his pacing long enough for her to slip the headcollar round his neck. As he was chewing his grain, she drew the noseband up over Zeebee's nose and fastened the headcollar. Then she distracted him with another handful of grain before sliding the reins over his head. Leaving him chewing for a moment, she quietly opened the gate to the field. Then she put both hands on Zeebee's back and, to his great surprise, hopped up and swung her leg over his back. It had been a long time since Zeebee had had a rider and it hadn't been a pleasant experience for him. He threw his head up in alarm.

Pandora may not have ever been a very nice rider, but she

was an experienced one. She gave Zeebee no time to react further to her sudden appearance on his back. Instead, she yanked his head around and pointed it at the gate before clapping her legs sharply into his sides. Zeebee gave a little rear and then bolted towards the gateway. In a flash, he was through it and galloping up the track in the direction that Duchess had taken Mark and Carlotta.

Pandora held on grimly. She quickly realised that this was not a horse who was happy with a rider. But it was too late. She was on him now and hurtling up the track out of control. Zeebee seemed barely aware she was there. He was in a blind panic.

They came to a sharp corner in the track. Zeebee executed a sharp turn. Pandora stayed with him initially, but the shift of her weight on the corner reminded him that there was a human on top of him. He suddenly realised that she was the cause of his fear. He pulled up and reared. This time it was a big rear, and he had every intention of throwing her off his back. He succeeded. Pandora fell to the ground with a thud. The noise of her hitting the ground set him off again. Tossing his head, he threw himself back into a fast dash up the mountainside, whinnying and calling as he went.

A little further on up the track he heard whinnies of reply from a herd of mountain ponies. Zeebee called and called to them, listening for their answers so he could work out how to get to them.

Covered in mud and broken heather, Pandora got up from the track and brushed herself down. She had lost the horse, was halfway up a mountain and had no idea where she was going. There was only one reasonable option for her, and that was to return to the castle. She could see it lit up from her position on the mountain, and the moonlight would make it possible to navigate the track back down to the castle. She felt annoyed that she hadn't been able to catch up with Mark and Carlotta, but she hadn't really fancied her chances of fighting Mark and kidnapping Carlotta single-handed anyway. The more she thought about it, the sillier the plan seemed.

Chapter 37

Mark was blissfully unaware that Zeebee was now missing. If he had known, he would have been horrified, although he might have felt better if he had known that Zeebee was now safely grazing the mountains with the wild herd of mountain ponies.

Instead, Mark and Carlotta were now at the Blue Caves. The first thing they had done was to make a rope corral for Duchess and settle her for the night. Fortunately, they had brought buckets and a tin of horse feed when they came last, so they were able to fetch water for her from a mountain stream nearby, and they would be able to give her a feed once she had cooled down.

"I think we should stay the night here," said Mark. "We don't know how that fight ended up down there or whether there are more Shadowlands ninjas around. I don't think they will come this far up the mountain, so we are safest here."

"You're right," agreed Carlotta. It's going to be cold here, but I would rather be cold than kidnapped! I only have to stay out of their hands one more day now so that my Father can get his Bill passed tomorrow. If they don't get me tonight, I am no use to them."

"That settles it!" declared Mark. "We will camp out here and go back tomorrow when the danger has passed. Sergeant Yeald knows where we are. They won't be worrying about us. Rather, I think they will be very relieved that we are here!"

Mark was very glad they had left torches at the cave. It was a bright moonlit night, but there was not enough light in the cave to see very much. Once they had managed to find the torches, they were then able to unpack enough equipment for the night. They made themselves comfortable bedding areas and found the gas stove, saucepan, soup and crackers.

Carlotta fished into one of the bags and drew out a large tin with a Christmas design on it. "Oh look! It's Lady Wallace's shortbread! I am glad we packed that!"

Mark laughed. "Good find! That would make a nice breakfast in the morning."

"Let's go and check on Duchess," suggested Carlotta. "She might be ready for something to eat now."

Duchess was very ready for her dinner. Although it was very dark now, it wasn't actually that late in the day. She would normally be having her last feed around now. She was delighted when Mark and Carlotta came out to see her and offered her the tin of grain.

"Good girl!" Mark stroked Duchess' neck as she ate from the tin that Carlotta was holding. "You got us away sure enough! What a heroine of a horse!"

"Thank you, Duchess," whispered Carlotta to her, leaning forward to kiss her forehead as she munched on the grain.

Once Duchess had been fed, and they were sure she had water and was happy enough, Mark and Carlotta returned to the cave. They considered lighting a fire to keep them warm, but Mark pointed out that it would create too much light and give their location away. Instead, they heated water on the stove to fill hot water bottles. They were glad that Sensei Tanaka had insisted on packing these. In fact, he had packed a dozen of them, so there were more than enough bottles to keep them warm under the bedding they made up for themselves.

Snuggled up under blankets, they sipped at soup that they had warmed on the stove, with only the light of a few candles to stave off the darkness. They may have been out of the wind in the cave, but it was a cruelly cold night. They were glad of the warmth of the soup, the blankets and the hot water bottles. The sky was clear, and the cave gave a magnificent view of the stars over the mountains and the Loch. They were gripping their hot water bottles and admiring the view as they drifted into sleep.

Chapter 38

After Mark and Carlotta had left the courtyard, the doors from the castle into the courtyard were flung open and out charged Lord Wallace and the Senseis. Like a wave of irresistible power, they flew around the courtyard, dispatching ninjas of all sizes in all directions. The Academy students drew back to the edges of the courtyard and watched in amazement as the three men went to work. They had seen quite a lot of martial arts by now, but nothing could have prepared them for this.

Sensei Goodwin was like a smiling whirlwind. As the ninjas attacked him, he span and flowed and sent them flying.

Sensei Tanaka was a more direct fighter. He was a flurry of flying hands and feet, punishing his attackers without damaging them, although he clearly could have if he had wanted.

Lord Wallace's fighting style of choice was with a long wooden staff. It reminded Charlie of the White Ninja the way he swept around and around, the staff appearing to glow as he cleared his attackers from his path.

Once free of the dozen ninjas who had targeted him, Sergeant Yeald also went into battle. His style was more police-like. He took up a piece of wood and wielded it like a baton, delivering sharp blows to the side of legs – not breaking them but causing them to be disabled with a single strike.

In a matter of minutes, the courtyard was clearing as the vanquished ninjas limped and crawled away. They knew they were defeated. They had thought they would just be fighting a group of twelve-year-olds and the Police Sergeant. But this had not turned out as they expected. They had lost the girl, got badly beaten and now were thoroughly defeated.

Once they started withdrawing, the Senseis, Lord Wallace and Sergeant Yeald let them go. They knew where they were from and what they had tried to do. It was enough that they were defeated. Nevertheless, the Senseis and Sergeant Yeald marched slowly after them as they retreated, making sure that they left by the road rather than attempting to go up the mountain where they might have found Mark and Carlotta.

When they returned to the castle, Sergeant Yeald wanted to go up the mountain to check on Mark and Carlotta. But he knew he could end up leading stray ninjas after them. So instead, he organised the students and the Senseis into shifts to patrol the area and make sure that there were no ninjas lingering to go after Carlotta again.

It was a long and cold night, but the students were all keen to play their part in this last phase of the operation. Taking it in turns to patrol or go back to warm up in the castle kitchen, they kept the watch going all through the night. The castle cook stayed up with them, making constant batches of hot tea, hot chocolate and cakes to keep them going.

With the morning, came the first fall of snow. Sergeant Yeald was pacing up and down in front of the castle now, feeling anxious for his charges. He was very relieved when he spotted a shape coming down the mountain track. As it drew closer, he could see it was Duchess carrying Mark and Carlotta.

"They are back!" he called out into the courtyard. All the students came running, some from their patrol duties and some from the castle kitchen. They all cheered as Duchess brought Mark and Carlotta back into the castle courtyard.

As they slipped off Duchess' back, Sergeant Yeald patted

Mark on the back. "Well done, old boy! Well done."

He had a tear in his eye. He hadn't realised how worried he had been until now, when he had both Mark and Carlotta safely back with him.

Lord Wallace came forward and took Duchess reins. He gave her a big hug, wrapping his arms around her massive neck. "Good girl!" he whispered in her ear. "Thank you very much."

Lord Wallace seemed to have forgotten about anyone else now. He was in a little world where only he and his big old horse existed. He led her away, talking to her in the warmest of tones, thanking her and telling her what an amazing horse she was. Xinia smiled. She understood this man.

"Come away inside! You will catch your death of cold!" Lady Wallace had appeared and was now shepherding everyone back into the castle. She wasn't happy until she had them all tucking into hearty breakfasts in the dining room with the log fire blazing.

Over breakfast, the students had much to talk about. Mark and Carlotta told the others about their flight up the mountain and about camping in the caves. The other students told them about the big battle with the ninjas and about what had happened at the end.

Then there was a silence. Everyone realised that Mark had to be told that Zeebee was missing, but nobody wanted to be the one to tell him. Knowing that he would be upset, they waited until he had finished his breakfast. Then it was Xinia that told him what had happened. She couldn't tell him everything, but she had seen her sister galloping off up the mountain on him and then later had seen her return without him. The rest could easily be guessed.

Mark looked stricken. Zeebee was missing?! He got up and ran out. Sergeant Yeald went after him. He knew that Mark would want to go after Zeebee.

"Look, Mark, there is no point. He will be away with the mountain ponies now. It's cold, it's snowing, and you have been through enough. You have to leave him be. He will return if that's what he wants to do."

Mark looked up at the Sergeant. "But anything could happen to him out there! I have to try and find him!"

The snow was falling thick and fast now. Sergeant Yeald

shook his head. "You won't find him. All you will achieve is freezing yourself to death and endangering any other horse you take. I don't often tell you what to do Mark, but I am telling you now. Your mother trusted me to look after you, and I can't let her down by letting you go up on that mountain in the snow. I'm sorry, but there it is, old boy. Now come back inside and warm up with a cup of tea."

Mark was torn between respect for the Sergeant and his love for the horse. He desperately wanted to go after Zeebee, but he knew that Sergeant Yeald was speaking good sense. Mark had no idea where Zeebee was. It was a big mountain range, and if he had joined up with a wild herd, they could be anywhere. He hung his head, blinking back the tears that threatened.

"Good lad." Sergeant Yeald patted him on the shoulder as he turned reluctantly back to the castle.

Chapter 39

After breakfast, Lady Wallace packed them all off to bed. "You've had a long, cold night and there will be a lot of aching bones after all that fighting. Off to bed with you all now!"

"But it's Christmas Eve!" protested Charlie.

"Even so!" declared Lady Wallace. "We have a fine, great, Christmas feast tonight. You won't want to be falling asleep and missing it now, will you?"

"What about the lighting of the Christmas tree candles?" asked Lucy who was very much looking forward to this.

"Well, there's no point in lighting them until it gets dark now, is there? Run along now and get some rest so you can enjoy all the celebrations tonight!" Lady Wallace practically swept the students from the room and off to bed.

Reluctantly, the students traipsed off to their rooms. They were still over excited by everything that had happened, but Lady Wallace was right. They were exhausted now, and there were a lot of yawns as they tumbled into bed.

261

Mark was the last to go to bed, though. He stood by the little window in the turret bedroom. It had a long view up the mountain and around one side of the Loch. He strained his eyes to try and see Zeebee. But the mountain was covered in a blanket of thick snow, and there was no sign of any horses. Yawning, he miserably turned from the window and got into his bed. He slept fitfully, tortured by nightmares about Zeebee.

Lady Wallace woke them all in the afternoon. "Time for baths and to clean yourselves up! I won't have any scruffy warriors at my Christmas table!"

She bustled around, organising baths for them all in various rooms in the castle. When all ablutions were complete, and Lady Wallace judged them presentable, it was time for afternoon tea and cakes. They were all drinking tea and waiting for the cakes to be brought in when the distinctive sound of helicopter blades was heard.

"Now I wonder who this could be?" Lady Wallace chuckled, relishing the surprise they had arranged for the students. "Shall we go and see?"

Everyone followed Lady and Lord Wallace out to greet the helicopter. It was the same massive military craft that had brought them up to Scotland a few weeks earlier. *How much has happened since then!* thought Mark.

The back of the helicopter dropped down and out came a crowd of people. First out was Norman Fairweather.

"Daddy!" Carlotta practically screamed; she was so excited and pleased to see him. She ran to her father and was welcomed by an engulfing hug.

"Goodness! Who is this?! I barely recognise you! Could this be my daughter?" He laughed and turned her around, delighted to see how well she looked. It had been a long time since he had seen her without crazy coloured hair, wild makeup and various extremes of costume.

Behind him, the parents of the various students emerged. Mark ran to his Mum, Xinia to her parents and David, Gina and Nell to theirs. Lucy was delighted to see that her Mum had come too. When all the other parents had emerged, she thought her mother might have had to stay at the Academy because she was the doctor. But here she was. Lucy hugged her Mum, really pleased to see her.

"I have got so much to tell you, Mum," she said.

Mark suddenly noticed that there was no-one here for Charlie. Charlie didn't look surprised, though. He beckoned Charlie over and introduced him to his mother. "This is Charlie, Mum. He is my best friend. He is going to be a police officer too!"

"Hello, Charlie. I am very pleased to meet you." Mark's mother greeted him with a warm smile. "Are your parents not here?"

Charlie looked slightly sad. "I don't have any parents, Mrs Vardy. They died when I was very young. It's just me now. I don't have a family."

"Oh, I am so sorry!" she replied sorrowfully. "Well, if you are Mark's best friend, you are part of our family now. Would you like that?"

Mark beamed. He was so proud of his Mum, who was the nicest person in the world and always had enough love to care for everyone who needed it.

Charlie smiled shyly. "I would like that very much, Mrs Vardy."

Mrs Vardy put one arm around Mark and the other around

Charlie. "Now, are you going to show me this magical castle you have been staying in?"

"Oh look! There is Mr Liu and Sensei Silver - and Professor Ballard!" cried Charlie.

"I know. I had the pleasure of getting to know them in the helicopter on the way up here," replied Mark's mother. "What lovely gentlemen! They all speak so highly of you all as well."

Mark and Charlie exchanged looks and giggled. They couldn't imagine their teachers saying nice things about them. They waved at Mr Liu, who came over to say hello.

"Hello, Mr Liu! Did you come for Christmas too?" asked Mark.

"I did! I wanted to come and see what you have been up to. You must tell me all about it. I hear you have been on more great adventures!"

"It has been brilliant!" declared Charlie. "We missed you, though. All that is missing here is Mr Liu and TigerLily!"

"I am here now! TigerLily couldn't make it, though. She is back at the Academy, but she will be very happy to see you when you get back."

Mr Liu walked into the castle with Mrs Vardy and the two boys as everyone went indoors for tea and cakes. More introductions were made, and there was much conversation about what had been happening.

"I have been so happy at the Academy Dad," Carlotta told her father. "I don't want to go back to London and having tutors. I want to go to school now. In fact, I really want to go to the Academy as a normal student."

"Well, I can see that it agrees with you," replied Norman. "Let me have a word with the headmaster, and we will see what can be done. But don't get your hopes up. This is a very special school indeed, and it is very hard to get in here. They have been doing us a big favour, you know."

"I know Dad, but will you ask? Please?" Carlotta was pleading now.

Norman Fairweather never thought he would see the day when his daughter begged to go to school. He could see that the Academy had had a tremendous effect on her. Gone was the sulky teen whose only interest seemed to be in making herself look strange. Now she clearly had friends and the headmaster had told him that she had engaged thoroughly in the Academy lessons. Apparently, she had even been riding horses again! She also looked healthy and normal. He couldn't see a single reason to object to her joining the Academy, but he didn't want to put any undue pressure on the headmaster. It wouldn't be fair after all they had done for her.

As he approached the headmaster, wondering how to raise the subject of his daughter's request, he was greeted with a big smile.

"Mr Fairweather! I am delighted to be able to hand your daughter back to you safe and sound. But there is something I would like to talk to you about if you don't mind?"

"Of course? What is it?" asked Norman.

"Well, I would like you to consider letting young Carlotta become a regular student at the Academy. We have been so impressed with her since she has been with us. She may not have attended our selection course, but we would have selected her if she had. She is brave, clever, works hard, faces her fears and overcomes them and is very talented at martial arts. She works well with the other students, has made friends with all of them, and when it came down to it, she apparently fought like a tiger when the Shadowlands ninjas attacked. We couldn't ask anything more from a student. I think she could have a great future with us." Professor Ballard made his case powerfully. He needn't have bothered though. Norman enjoyed hearing all this of course and smiled broadly.

"Funny you should mention it, that's exactly what I wanted to talk to you about! Carlotta implored me to ask if she could stay on at the Academy."

"Well, that's that settled then," Professor Ballard said with a laugh. "Will you let her know, or shall I?"

"If you don't mind Professor, I would rather enjoy telling her myself. She has been through so much and done so well. I am very proud of her and want to tell her." Norman Fairweather shook the headmaster's hand and went off to tell Carlotta, who was hovering by the window and watching.

Before he could break the good news to Carlotta, Lord and Lady Wallace announced that it was time to light the Christmas tree in the courtyard.

Chapter 40

The lighting of the Christmas tree was a joyous affair. As promised, the students were allowed to do the lighting of the candles, using long tapers and sticks to reach the upper branches. When all the candles were lit, the Christmas tree was a sight to behold. It twinkled with the light of more than a hundred little candles which lit the faces of all as they stood around it and sang Christmas Carols.

Mark looked up at his Mum and around at his friends, their hosts, Mr Liu and the Senseis. This would be a moment of perfect happiness if it were not for one thing – well two things, but he had long since accepted that his Father could never be here to share such moments. Zeebee was a new loss though and he was far from accepting it. He hadn't told his Mum about Zeebee yet. He didn't know where to start, and it was a long story. But he looked longingly out of the courtyard into the snowy mountain beyond, wishing and willing Zeebee to appear.

Xinia caught his eye. She knew exactly what he was thinking and smiled sympathetically. She could hardly imagine losing her horse Rainbow like that. Mark must be in agony!

When the Carols were finished, and the tree had been thoroughly admired and appreciated, Lady Wallace invited everyone to come into the Grand Dining Room for the Christmas Feast. Everyone crowded eagerly indoors and into the dining room. The long table groaned under the weight of a magnificent spread of every type of beautiful food. The table decorations that the students had made were arranged between food platters, and the candles within them were twinkling amongst the delicious looking dishes.

Lady Wallace invited everyone to take a seat and enjoy the sumptuous feast laid out for them. She didn't have to ask them twice. A dozen hungry students, their parents, Senseis, Mr Liu and Sergeant Yeald all happily sat down to enjoy the meal.

Over dinner, Mark told his Mother and Mr Liu all about Zeebee, how he had met him, how Lord Wallace had invited him to help with his training and about all the time he had spent with the horse. His eyes were misty as he talked about his first contact with Zeebee and the trust that had developed between them.

"But now he is gone," finished Mark after explaining the events of the previous night. "And I don't even know he is

270

safe. I might never see him again. Anything could have happened to him."

Mr Liu listened to all this without saying a word. He just nodded in understanding, encouraging Mark to tell everything. When Mark stuttered to a stop with his tale, Mr Liu finally spoke.

"A horse is a wild creature at heart, Mark. They lend us their power and gift us with their presence, but the call of the wild is the strongest call of all. He will be with the wild herd now. Maybe he will stay with them; maybe he will return. But he will be true to his nature and his heart. You mustn't be sad for him. He will choose what his life will hold now. This is how it should be."

Mark tried to understand. He could hear Mr Liu's words, and he knew him well enough to know that he was a man of great wisdom. But his heart could only feel one thing, and that was an unbearable sense of loss.

There was a tinkling sound as Mr Fairweather got to his feet and tapped his knife to his glass to get everyone's attention.

"Thank you, everyone. In fact, I have a lot of thank-yous to say. First of all, I would like to thank the Academy for taking Carlotta in at our hour of need. I understand that her classmates have been dedicated and fantastic bodyguards, so I would like to thank you all very much for looking after Carlotta and keeping her safe for me. You have gone above and beyond the call of duty and I am so very grateful for all you have done. Thank you also to your Senseis and to Sergeant Yeald, who have done so much to help us. And thank you to Lord and Lady Wallace for accommodating all of these wonderful people and for this fantastic feast tonight!"

"Hear, hear!" everyone called, and there was a big round of applause.

"Before I give way to our wonderful hosts, I have a couple of pieces of news for you all. Firstly, I am delighted to share the news that Carlotta has been invited to become a regular student at the Academy! I cannot begin to tell you how happy and proud that makes me."

All the students rose to their feet, clapping and cheering. Professor Ballard smiled. He knew he had made a good decision, and it was nice to see how pleased her classmates were.

"Well done, Carlotta!" called Mark.

Lucy gave Carlotta a big smile. "Didn't I tell you it would all work out!"

Norman Fairweather continued. "Thank you all for making Carlotta so welcome and taking her in as one of your own. I know she will be very happy with you. Now I have one more piece of news. As you know, the reason Carlotta came to be with you was to keep her safe, so that I could usher a very important Bill through Parliament. Well, I am delighted to tell you that the vote went in favour today. The Bill was successful, and your freedom of speech is now protected in law! You did it! You made this possible!"

Everyone was on their feet now, and the applause was thunderous. After all that they had been through, their mission had been successful.

"Well done, everyone! Very well done indeed!" Norman raised a glass and toasted everyone who had made this possible.

When the applause settled down, Lord Wallace took to his feet. "It has been wonderful having you all to stay with us. I hope you will all consider this your home from home now. You are all extremely welcome any time. And to help you remember us and your time here, Lady Wallace and I have had some special gifts made for you."

Lord Wallace gestured to a couple of servants who were waiting nearby holding large silver trays on which sat small blue velvet boxes. They went along the table, setting a box before everyone there.

"Go ahead! Open them!" Lord Wallace encouraged. All the guests opened their box, and inside they found a small piece of glittering blue crystal that had been mounted on a necklace.

Lucy's eyes lit up. She recognised that crystal! She was so happy that she could show her mother what she had been telling her about earlier. Even better, her mother had her own piece of crystal too!

Lord Wallace chuckled at her delighted response to the gift. "Yes, Lucy! You each have a small piece of the blue crystal from the Blue Caves. Now you can wear it and remember your Scottish adventures wherever you are in the world and wherever life takes you."

"Thank you!" cries of thanks came from all around the

table and the students all put their necklaces on immediately, delighted with how well they looked against their black outfits.

"Now we look like a very special ninja squad!" exclaimed Charlie.

It was time for the Christmas puddings to be served next. Large puddings were brought in and placed on the table. Whisky was poured over them, and they were set alight, to the delight of all. Then it was served with a special cream made of almonds, with mince pies on the side.

Mark was enjoying all this, but his heart was still heavy. His Mum watched him, a little worried for him. She knew him so well. He was so like his Father, hiding his pain and pretending everything was fine when it really wasn't inside. She wished there was something she could do to make this better for him and privately prayed that everything would turn out for the best.

No sooner had the prayer left her mind than there was a sound coming from the courtyard. It was the sound of horse's hooves on the flagstones. Lord Wallace looked up. There shouldn't have been any horses out there at this time. Mark was on his feet in a flash. He ran to the window, and his heart was filled with pure joy. Standing there by the Christmas tree, lit by the candlelight, was a black and white horse. Zeebee had returned!

Mark ran from the window, out of the dining room and out into the courtyard. "Zeebee!" he cried softly. The horse gave a long low whicker and went to him, pressing his face to Mark's chest. Mark put his arms around Zeebee's head and pressed a kiss to the fluffy black and white forelock and into his forehead. "You came back!"

As Mark stood there hugging the little horse, his friends, family, and other guests poured quietly into the courtyard. They were all extremely happy for Mark and to see Zeebee safely returned.

Lord Wallace stepped forward. "He came back to you, Mark, do you realise that?"

"Yes, he came back," Mark whispered into Zeebee's mane as he hugged him.

"No, I mean he came back to you, nobody else. He has chosen you as his person."

"Do you think so?" asked Mark in wonder.

"Absolutely. A horse is a creature of the heart. When he gives his heart, it is yours for life. Mark, Zeebee is your horse now."

Mark's mouth dropped open in amazement. "Really? Zeebee is mine? He is my horse?"

Lord Wallace backed away, nodding slowly and letting the realisation sink in.

Mark felt his eyes well up with emotion. He wrapped his arms around Zeebee's neck and hugged him again. "It's you and me now, Zeebee. You are my horse, and I am your human. Thank you so much for coming back to me."

Mark felt the strangest of feelings at that moment. It was as if a bolt of golden light had shot from his chest into Zeebee's and been reflected back. Bonded to his horse now and filled with the purest and warmest of love, he looked around and smiled to see that his Mum and all his friends and Senseis were sharing this moment with him. They smiled back at him. Xinia winked to let him know that she knew exactly what had just happened.

High above on the rooftops, a mysterious, silent figure looked down on the scene below. Without alerting anyone to their presence, the figure withdrew and melted into the Christmas night.

THE END

Sign up for the Mark Vardy newsletter for all the news and updates:

https://www.markvardy.com

READ BOOK 3 IN THE MARK VARDY SERIES!

MARK VARDY
AND THE
STAFF OF LIGHT

Mark Vardy returns to the elite and secretive Martial Arts Academy and once again must take on the evil forces of the Shadowlands Ninjas. This time, it is even more serious and Mark is shocked at the lengths his foes will go to. Can Mark and his friends stand against their grab for supreme power?

The Shadowlands organisation has discovered that the mysterious Staff of Light wielded by the Academy's White Ninja may be an all-powerful historic artifact that has empowered kings and rulers for centuries. They will stop at nothing to obtain it. Someone could get hurt - badly hurt. Will Mark and his friends learn the secret of the Staff of Light and the source of its power? Will they keep it from falling into the hands of the wicked Shadowlands organisation?

In this third book in the Adventures of Mark Vardy series, Mark learns about the power of resilience and the importance of getting up, no matter how many times you are knocked down.

HAVE YOU READ BOOK 1 IN THE MARK VARDY
SERIES?

MARK VARDY
AND THE
SCHOOL OF NINJAS

Twelve-year-old Mark Vardy has always looked up to his policeman father. That's why he formed his own junior police force. When Mark started arresting real criminals, he received an unexpected invitation to try for a place at The Academy - a select martial arts institution in England's beautiful New Forest that hones the skills and spirit of a new generation of heroes.

Mark makes interesting new friends at The Academy, as he trains in the mysteries and secrets of the martial arts. But sinister students from the rival Shadowlands School of Ninjas begin plotting a nefarious scheme that will truly test the mettle of Mark and his classmates.

When Mark's future, dreams and ambitions are at stake, can Mark keep his commitment to doing the right thing? And when the loyalty of friends is tested, which of his fellow Warriors-in-training will remain at his side?

THE MARK VARDY SERIES

TO BE CONTINUED...

ABOUT THE AUTHOR

C.J.T. Wilkins is a Martial Artist and instructor, living in the New Forest, Hampshire, England.

A wearer of many hats.

Printed in Great Britain
by Amazon

61897829R00168